Leather and Grit

DRAWING THE DEVIL

JON KEYS

Drawing the Devil
ISBN # 978-1-913186-19-7
©Copyright Jon Keys 2017
Cover Art by Posh Gosh ©Copyright December 2017
Interior text design by Claire Siemaszkiewicz
Pride Publishing

Published in 2019 by Pride Publishing, United Kingdom.

Pride Publishing books by Jon Keys

Single Books
Showstring
Crossfire
Tackling the Subject
A Matter of Priorities
Construction

Leather and Grit
Drawing the Devil
Wrestling with Destiny
Roping in his Heart

Anthologies
Right Here, Right Now: Throwaway

DRAWING
THE DEVIL

Chapter One

Shane stared at the mirror, trying again to paint a smile onto his almost-perpetual frown. *But my job is all about the entertainment. Reality has nothing to do with it. Okay, there is the whole line about saving the cocky bull riders who aren't as good as they think they are — none of them.* He shook himself like a terrier shakes a rat and refocused on finishing the façade he was creating.

He couldn't keep from glancing around the room the fairgrounds provided for him and the other bullfighters to use as a staging area. It reminded Shane more of a jail cell in some backwoods county, with its smell of stale urine and mildew that filled his senses. Shane had been doing his routine as a bullfighter since his days in the peewee rodeos where his job had consisted of making sure other kids weren't banged up too bad when the small bulls-in-training tossed them on their asses.

"You drew him again."

Shane grinned at the echo of himself he saw in the mirror. He jumped from his seat and wrapped his arms around his twin brother. The two embraced tightly before Shane hesitantly released Sam. Shane felt he was under microscopic scrutiny as his brother gazed from one new scar to another, but he was relieved when Sam gave him no more response than a melancholy smile.

"What?"

"I haven't seen you in a long time. We thought you'd come home for winter and spend time with us," Sam said.

Shane's mood shifted to a darker place at the mention of his family. "Why would that seem like a good idea? Mom doesn't need more time to have her friends from church pray for me and Dad doesn't have to be more disappointed with his gay son. It isn't worth the drama."

"They aren't that bad." Sam glanced at his brother and sighed. "Well, they're getting better."

Shane shrugged and sat with a frown. He studied his brother for a long minute before saying anything, but by then, his curiosity had gotten the better of him. "Why are you here? I was shocked to get your text."

"I haven't heard from you in six months. Sara has to keep everyone updated. Our sister is fearless and loves you, but you need to give the rest of us a chance."

Shane turned away from his brother and continued applying his clown face. The quiet became heavy before Shane pointed out the obvious. "I'm thrilled Sara is fighting for me, but you didn't answer my question. Why did you make a three-hundred-mile road trip from the ranch to show up at this little rodeo?"

Sam scowled but answered this time. "Dad sent me to check out the bulls from a ranch northwest of Lawton.

I visited them then high-tailed it up here to see with you while you're close. I do love you, older brother."

Shane grinned but kept applying his paint. "Ten minutes' difference. You're ten minutes younger. Why don't you get over here and do something useful, like helping with my makeup?"

Sam chuckled, moved a stool beside Shane and pulled the makeup to him. He took the sponge from Shane and evened out a few spots on the white base before working around Shane's eyes. The deft strokes of the brush hid a lot of Shane's scarring, but not all of it by any stretch of the imagination. They sat in silence for several minutes as Sam worked on the application.

"You're in the arena with him again. You knew it would happen."

Shane sighed. "Yeah, I'm in the arena with the bull who fucked up my face and almost did me in."

There was another pause in the conversation while Sam applied the last of the paint to his satisfaction. He leaned back to admire his work. "You know, it was fun when the two of us were bullfighters together."

Shane chuckled as he peered into the mirror at his brother. "First, your wife would kill both of us because it would somehow be my fault. Then the parental units wouldn't be happy either. It would be a lose-lose situation."

"Well, a guy can live vicariously through his brother's glamorous life."

Shane snorted. "Help me with the outfit. It should be interesting to see if Diablo finishes what he started."

Chapter Two

Nothing made Dustin feel more alive than lasting eight seconds on a ton of beef and balls that ate cowboys for lunch. The rush was almost as good as sex. Almost. The bull he'd drawn today should leave him with one hell of a buzz. A vicious bull that took on all comers, it stormed down the chute searching for anyone or anything within the reach of his horns to unleash his vile temperament on.

"Get him in there, boys!" yelled Dustin.

His pulse raced as the bull slammed into the gate, never slowing from his headlong sprint down the alleyway. The enraged animal tried to climb over the chute, hooves banging against the enclosure. Dustin waited for an instant of stillness then dropped onto the brindle hide below him. The metal chute was tight as Dustin wrapped his legs around the bull with no room to spare. His body flooded with adrenaline as he tried to read one of the meanest bulls on the circuit. He yanked the rope around his rosin-coated glove as Diablo fought with the chute then drew his crotch snug against his hand. As his last act of preparation, Dustin rammed his cowboy hat down tight. He sensed the millisecond when everything aligned. He gave the gateman a quick flip of his head, signaling for all hell to be released.

The side of the chute flew open with the force of two thousand pounds of muscle slamming against it, ending with the crash of metal against metal. The bull jumped sideways to clear the gate by inches before dropping into a spin.

With a snap of his hindquarters, the animal sprinted a few yards, then contracted like the devil's slinky. It uncoiled violently, slashing the air with all four hooves in a gravity-defying maneuver. As he fought to expect each of the bull's battle strategies, Dustin tightened his jaw in determination. The beast finished his latest jump by slamming against the ground, jarring Dustin to the bone.

Fuck! I see why this bastard's named Diablo.

The bull dropped into another whirl. His body swapped ends with each thump of Dustin's heart. As the bull hit his stride, Dustin struggled to regain control. *No! Fuck! You aren't tossing me.* As the bull seemed to sense Dustin's effort, it flipped back on itself and reversed the spin. The forces pummeled Dustin as he struggled to maintain his grip with every muscle in his body. In spite of his talent and strength of will, the force of nature he tried to ride became overwhelming. His battle against both bull and time ended as he fell into the hellish vortex the animal had created.

Shane's gut had twisted when the gate had exploded outward and a familiar tiger-striped bull had jumped into the arena. *It had to be this motherfucker?* In an unconscious action, he'd touched the thick scar bisecting his face—a souvenir from the last time he'd danced with this bull. The crash of metal against metal as it burst from the chute had signaled the start of Shane's job. All thoughts of himself had faded as he'd focused his entire being on the cowboy who might need his help.

Shane had tracked everyone as he'd positioned himself—rider, bullfighters and bull. There was a reason this animal had won the vote for being the meanest at most of the rodeos he was at. Diablo liked to hurt cowboys and bullfighters. It declared open season on everyone and everything from the instant he entered the arena.

Shane had gathered up the tattered legs of his costume to prepare for quick movement as he'd read the beast's moves. He'd known he had to adjust his position constantly so he could rush in if needed.

He'd studied the rider and how he'd handled the bull through the first jumps. Shane could imagine the teeth-rattling impact reverberating through the cowboy when the bull had ended one maneuver to begin another. The cowboy seemed close to winning the battle this time when it happened—the break in rhythm marking the rider's loss of dominance. *Damn it.* Shane ran toward the bull. This rider would need help to get out of the arena with all his bits intact. Shane shifted into a frantic sprint when the cowboy lost his seat and fell into Diablo's violent spin.

Shane waved his hands as he ran to intercept the animal, hoping the loose flags of clothing would distract the bull from the cowboy trying to keep a failing grip. A split second later, the situation snapped from bad to worse when the cowboy tangled in his bull rope. The slender rider bounced against the enraged animal's side like a hapless ragdoll.

Shit!

Shane ran across the rampant beast's path, hoping he would give one of the other bullfighters enough time to get there. "Come on, you worthless piece of hamburger meat. Chase me!"

The bull spun toward Shane, responding to the rag streamers flapping from his arms. Diablo pawed the arena floor, sending a plume of fine dust high into the haze-filled air then charged Shane. As he ran a diagonal path in front of it, another bullfighter yanked on the kid's arm. The cowboy popped loose from the rigging and the pair landed in a twisted pile on the packed dirt while Shane raced past. He dodged the end of Diablo's blunt horn by inches as he danced away, leading the animal from the pair struggling to get across the expanse and to safety.

Shane raced toward the barrelman, who dropped inside at his approach. As the man's painted face disappeared, Shane spun the barrel and positioned it between himself and the bull. Not a heartbeat later, it charged and a dull *thud* sounded as a cockeyed horn struck the barrel's aluminum wall. Diablo paused then dug his hoof into the powder covering the ground under them and launched another spire of dust before charging Shane.

Shit! What's taking so long? Get that cowboy out of here!

Shane gauged the others' progress as he worked to keep the barrel between himself and the lethal animal. After the test of will, the beast snorted again before running along the wall with his tail held in a stiff arch. Shane used the time to catch his breath. But time was in hyper gear and it seemed only a heartbeat passed before he circled back and spotted a new target. Diablo's head snapped up, his nostrils flared and he spun toward the fleeing pair.

Goddamn it!

It thundered toward them as they ran for the gate. The chance of Shane intercepting the ton of furious bull didn't exist, but he refused to give up without a fight. He ran at Diablo, elated when the monster whirled toward him again. The certain result was a collision course, with a pissed-off bull the undeniable winner. A hundred different choices flashed through Shane's head, but the only one with a chance of not getting him killed relied on how well his body remembered his years of running track and competing in gymnastics.

Oh, hell. Here we go again.

A gasp erupted from the crowd when, at the last second, Shane changed directions and jumped toward the bull.

Diablo did some combination of spinning, jumping and slamming on the brakes as Shane's foot landed on its head. His momentum carried Shane forward to land several yards beyond the animal's ass end. The crowd jumped to their feet and erupted into thunderous applause. He spun in time to see the cowboy yanked over the fence. The other bullfighter ran back into the arena as the bull shot out of the gate.

Shane walked to the barrelman and slapped him on the back. "Did you get a nice nap in there? Ready for another set of balls attached to a bull who wants to make you as ugly as I am?"

His friend shook his head. "You're fucking crazy, Shane."

The crowd erupted into thunderous applause. Shane threw up his arms in a triumphant gesture and curtseyed.

The rides left in today's round were nothing compared to the drama with Diablo and the skinny kid who'd come so close to riding him. For the most part, they consisted of him handing the cowboy his hat back.

He thought he'd spotted the kid a few times outside the fences, but Shane found his interest at the end of the night was more aimed at the nearest bar for a glass of cold beer and a plate of whatever passed as food. Shane wasn't sure he could take the drunken thanks of another pretty eighteen-year-old. At this point, the beer and food were his first priority — the other he'd deal with when it happened.

Chapter Three

Shane sat in a dark corner of the bar, the intermittent flashes of neon the only illumination. He and Sam had shared a meal earlier to the blaring thrum of country music so his twin could start the trip back to the family ranch north of Lubbock. Once he and his twin had shared their goodbyes, he'd settled in with his beer to do some serious people watching. Otherwise, his focus now comprised washing the taste of arena out of his mouth. He was engrossed with the sight of a bull rider getting shot down by one of the local girls when someone tapped his shoulder. He turned to find the kid who'd tried to ride Diablo.

"Hey, man. I'm Dustin. You saved my ass today. Your drinks are on me. They said you jumped the damn bull to give them time to drag me out. That's fucking amazing, man."

Shane lifted his glass, filled his mouth with the cool amber liquid then let it slide down his dry throat as their eyes met. "Name's Shane. Glad to meet you and that we got you out intact. You drew the nastiest bull on the circuit. Don't feel like you owe me anything, though. Just doing my job."

"No way are you getting off that easy. The beer's on me — no doubt about it."

Shane smirked a bit at his next question. "Are you even twenty-one?"

Dustin puckered his mouth but his voice didn't betray his thoughts like his facial expression did. "Yes, I'm twenty-one. Going on twenty-two."

Shane nodded and took another sip before answering. "Good, because with the amount of beer I plan to drink tonight, it'll cost you."

Dimples appeared in Dustin's cheeks when he grinned. "I ended up winning today, so I can cover it."

Shane found himself leaning deeper into the shadows. The kid was making him more aware of his scarred face than normal. He hoped to cut this conversation short — if he was lucky. "You won? I thought you fell before the buzzer?"

Dustin lifted his beer to his lips, pausing, then taking several deep swigs from the bottle. Shane couldn't help but notice Dustin's prominent Adam's apple dancing as he swallowed.

The kid's kind of hot.

Dustin lowered his almost-empty bottle with a sigh. "Everyone had shitty rides today, but my other go-rounds kicked ass, so I ended up with the high score."

Another cocky, good-looking bull rider... Great.

"Hey, fag, how's it going'?"

Shane bristled, getting ready to defend himself, but then realized the slur was directed at Dustin.

"Yeah, idiot. Whose ass is talking for him again?" Dustin responded.

The newcomer tilted his hat and graced them with a friendly wink. "Yeah, whatever. We'll see who's packing more junk. Just wait."

"Hey, asshole, meet Shane. He's the bullfighter who saved my butt today. We were just talking about how much beer he'd have to drink before we're even." Dustin turned to Shane. "This is my lifelong friend and general jackass, Todd."

"Yeah, whatever. Dustin just has fantasies about what's in my jeans."

"You're such a dumb shit."

"Yeah, I need to find some hot tail for tonight."

"Go for it. You might find a chick here who'll think you rate high enough for a one-night stand."

Todd flipped Dustin off as he walked toward a huddle of girls whose drinks all had tiny umbrellas.

Dustin twisted back to Shane. "Sorry about Todd. He's an ass, but he's my best friend." Dustin drained the last sip of beer from his longneck, signaled the bartender for another and drank from the frosty bottle when he brought it. "He's also my closest competition."

"Yeah, I understood you were high in the earnings. Did you decide to take a run at finals?"

Dustin nodded and set down his beer. "Yup. I've got a good shot at making the short list if I don't get too many more repeats of today."

Shane touched the deep scar. "Yeah, Diablo's a bad son of a bitch."

Dustin shot forward, grabbed Shane's chin and turned his face toward the light. The silence between them stretched on as Dustin studied Shane's scar. His eyebrows furrowed when he met Shane's gaze again. "He did that? Nasty SOB. He should be dog food."

Shane reached up, lifted Dustin's hand away and tried not to show how much the intimacy bothered him.

He leaned against the wall and glowered at Dustin. *Arrogant ass. I'm not some freak for your inspection.*

Dustin didn't seem to notice as he motioned for the bartender. "Hey, my buddy needs another beer." A fresh bottle appeared on the bar in front of Shane. Dustin continued to flit from topic to topic without pause, and Shane realized the incident with his scar had been no more meaningful to Dustin than the color of the wall. Social skills didn't seem to be one of Dustin's strong points, but as the night wore on, Shane found more and more that Dustin's bluntness was a charming quirk rather than an offensive annoyance.

"So yeah, I was like 'get your skanky ass off me', and her nasty tongue wagged out of her mouth like a baby calf after a bottle. I mean—" Dustin shoved his tongue out as far as possible and waved it in the air.

Shane held his side, sore from an evening of laughing at Dustin and his wild stories. The time made Shane more comfortable with someone other than his siblings than he'd been in years. He finished the last swallow of the second bottle Dustin had bought for him. Shane knew his limit. He needed to be several hundred miles north of here and across some state lines before he stopped for the night.

The last thing I need is a DUI.

He motioned to Dustin so he could be heard over the din. "Sorry to cut this short, but I'd better go. I have to be in Cody tomorrow."

"Hey, that's my next rodeo, too. Todd was driving, but he's decided to hit the one in New Mexico. I was going to catch a ride with one of the other bull riders, but would you mind if I bum a lift? I'll split the gas and motel room. That'll save us some money. I don't know about you, but I wouldn't mind having some extra cash in my pocket when I arrive there."

Shane studied him for a few seconds and considered how comfortable he'd become with Dustin. "That'll work. You don't mind sharing a room?"

"Nope. Sounds solid. I'm about done here. We can get on the road and put some distance behind us before stopping for the night." Dustin stretched and stifled a yawn. "Not too far, though. I'm already beat. You good to drive?"

Shane nodded. "Yeah, I was a cheap hero for you. I only had a couple of beers all night. Let's head out. We couldn't find a motel around here, anyway. They're all booked for the ending celebrations of the rodeo."

"Cool. Let me tell Todd."

Shane nodded, glad he hadn't agreed to travel with both Dustin and Todd. Their juvenile banter would get old fast. Dustin by himself had the potential to wear on his nerves as it was. The kid might find himself breaking in a pair of boots by walking down a Kansas highway.

Shane followed a few steps behind as Dustin searched for his friend. Then Dustin shot off toward the small group of bull riders where he'd seen Todd. They greeted each other with a fist bump and an appropriate bro hug.

"Hey, Todd, I'm jettin'. I'll leave my pickup at your place until your dad has time to check it out," Dustin said.

Todd nodded as he leaned in to give the curvy blonde under his arm a kiss on the cheek. "That's cool. You found a ride, then?"

"Yup," Dustin motioned over his shoulder toward Shane. "Shane's going to the same rodeo, so I'm sharing a ride with him. We're gonna drive as long as we can then crash for the night."

The band started their next set and Shane wouldn't have been able to hear the conversation unless they were screaming in his ear. But he didn't have to hear whatever was being said between the two bull riders to tell that Dustin wasn't pleased with the direction the discussion was going.

After a couple of animated exchanges—some of which seemed to include him—Dustin flipped Todd off with both hands and headed back to Shane. He didn't seem happy as he walked past Shane and motioned him to follow.

Once they were in the relative quiet of the bar's parking lot, Dustin scowled at the building they had just left. "Todd's an asshole. I'm ready to go."

It didn't take long to toss all of Dustin's gear into Shane's pickup and begin the trip north. The conversation was less relaxed than Shane wanted, but he soon came to the conclusion that the discussion with Todd hadn't gone as Dustin had hoped. An hour into the drive, soft snoring was coming from Dustin. Shane didn't mind.

Shane figured they had traveled as far as possible when his yawns became huge and frequent. He pulled in to a hotel and Dustin jerked awake when Shane's pickup came to a stop.

"What's up?" Dustin asked as he rubbed his eyes.

"I can't drive any more tonight. I'll get us a room."

Shane jumped out of the truck, made his way through the deserted lobby and rang the bell. A few seconds later the clerk's smiling face appeared. "Evening, gentlemen. What can I do for you?"

"We need a double room for the night."

There were several minutes of quiet followed by flurries of typing. With a frown and a shake of his head, the clerk turned back to Shane.

"Sorry, sir. The only room I have left is a single."

Shane let out a deep sigh and tapped a rapid rhythm on the dark countertop of the motel's desk with his fingers. "You're sure? One single?"

"Yes, sir. Sorry. The state high school softball tournament is in town and all accommodations are booked."

Why does this crap always happen to me?

Shane glanced at Dustin, concerned about what the rodeo rumor mill might make of the situation. He'd have to tell Dustin about himself. It wasn't fair otherwise. "What do you think? I can sleep in the chair or something," said Shane.

"Nah, we can share the bed. The clerk said it's a queen. I'm beat. I don't want to drive any farther."

"Yeah, me either. I want to wash the dirt off me and crash."

"Okay."

Shane turned to the desk clerk, completed the arrangements then handed Dustin his key card. A few minutes later found them standing at their door with Dustin struggling to get the lock's magic green light to appear. Each time the light flashed red, Dustin's curses increased in volume and crudeness. After a final frustrated swipe, he unlocked it and shoved the door open. They tossed their stuff onto the one bed and Shane surveyed the room. *Spartan but functional.* He glanced in the bathroom. "It's clean. I've slept in worse. I'll take a quick shower then you can have it. That work for you?"

"Sure. I'll just chill and see if there's anything on the tube." Dustin grabbed the remote and a few seconds later images flashed past on the television like a bad vacation slide show. He flipped through channels so fast that Shane couldn't imagine how he could tell what he was seeing. Shane cocked his head when Dustin stopped at Cartoon Network and lay back on the bed to watch. Too exhausted to worry about offending Dustin, Shane undressed, tossing his clothes into a pile before starting the shower. He would have sworn Dustin was watching, but as Shane drew the bathroom door closed, Dustin's attention seemed riveted on a Road Runner cartoon.

The heat of the water soaked into his sore muscles. *Damn, what a hell of a day. It seems like I've been doing this since I was fourteen.* Shane spent several delicious minutes letting the hot spray loosen some of his aches. *I shouldn't be this bruised after a night in the arena. For God's sake, I'm just twenty-six but tonight I feel more like sixty-six.*

Shane squirted some of the motel soap on the thin washcloth. He washed himself, happy with the definition he'd kept from all those years of gymnastics. *That stuff saved my bacon today.* He shook his head as he rinsed, running the washcloth over his chest and stomach.

He slipped his hands around his cock and stroked it a few times. The slight erection he got left him with a smile. *At least that still works.* The hot water had loosened his tense muscles enough that he enjoyed the tingle that coursed through his body when the dripping cloth ran over his pucker. He stood for a last few minutes, thinking about Dustin and how he'd enjoyed their time. *Too bad it can't last.*

Shane emerged from the shower to find Dustin still glued to the television. He rubbed the towel over his hair then wrapped it around his waist. He turned his back to Dustin to dig through his bag for a toothbrush to finish his nightly routine. "Shower's all yours."

Dustin tossed the remote on the bed, bounced around and gaped at Shane. "Damn! What happened to you?"

Shane shot his hand to his facial scar before he realized Dustin's eyes were locked on the livid marks across his ribs. He let out a sigh of relief as he answered. "A bull was too fast for me a year or so ago. He caught me with his horn on a day I was too stupid to wear a vest." Shane met Dustin's gaze. "Bull riders aren't the only ones who suffer from immortality disease."

Dustin's eyes twinkled. "Yeah, bull riders are kinda full of themselves." He rolled to his back, scooted his jeans and underwear off his ass and tossed them into a pile beside his bag.

Shane appreciated the brief show when Dustin's smooth butt appeared. Dustin windmilled his feet in the air, yanked off his socks and exposed his ass crack to Shane.

Fuck, he's sexy. Damn bull riders!

Dustin jumped to the floor, slipped his T-shirt over his head and shot it across the room as he bounded into the bathroom.

Oh my Lord. He's hyper.

Shane stepped into the dressing area across from the bathroom and wiped the steam off the mirror. As he laid out his shaving stuff, Dustin started singing. Shane squirted shaving cream into his hand as Dustin belted out one of the latest country songs. He spread it on his face, careful not to get too close to the scar. He inspected it closely, happy he no longer had to endure the vivid red color he'd lived with for months. *God must have a sense of humor. First he decides I'll be gay, then he scars me so no man will ever want me.*

Shane picked up the straight razor and scraped off his day's thick growth. While he shaved his neck, he couldn't help but hum along as Dustin belted out another song. It didn't take long for Shane to cut the whiskers from his face, clean the razor and store it away. Once everything was accomplished, he pulled the towel from his waist and finished all the nooks and crannies on his body that he'd missed earlier. He lifted one leg to dry the final spot.

Dustin stepped out of the shower and started toweling off. "Whoa, dude! Full ass-crack alert!"

Shane bundled his towel against his crotch. "Sorry."

"No problem. I don't like wearing clothes, but a loose pecker bugs Todd, so I try to keep it under wraps when we share a room."

Dustin flipped the towel he was using across his neck and danced around the tiny room, humming the song he'd been singing. Crawling onto the bed, Shane kept the towel over his crotch so Dustin couldn't see that his cock had hardened at the sight of him gyrating across the floor.

After a few minutes, Dustin dropped on the bed beside Shane. "You sure airing out my junk isn't bothering you? I can put on briefs if you want."

Shane popped his fingers playfully against Dustin's shoulder. "It's fine. I did gymnastics through high school. I'm used to guys walking around in their birthday suits."

"Cool." Dustin scooted so he leaned against the headboard and flipped through the channels again. His hand rested on his crotch, fingers trailing through his light-colored pubic hair.

To keep from staring, Shane checked the schedule the organizers had sent him and updated the paperwork on his computer. Dustin flipped channels like a mad man, never pausing for more than a few seconds. Eventually, he clicked the television off and tossed the remote to the nightstand. He stared over Shane's shoulder for a few minutes until Shane stopped and turned to him.

"What's up?"

Dustin winked at Shane. "Got any porn on there?"

Shane went as tense as a fiddle string. *Do I tell him? All I need is a freaked-out straight boy who thinks I'm seducing him.* Shane ran through his options for a few seconds and decided that while he might not be as out as he'd like, he refused to go backward, even to prevent drama with a cute bull rider.

"I don't think any porn I'd have would do much for you."

Dustin scratched his jaw. "Why? You into some kinky shit or something?"

"Dustin, I'm gay."

"Oh! Is that all? Hey, it's cool."

Shane studied the younger man. *Did he understand what I said? Maybe that's it?* "I understand if it makes you uncomfortable. I can sleep in the chair or something if it bothers you."

"Why, you gonna try to tap this ass?" Dustin grinned at Shane and patted his bare butt. Dustin's expression had Shane chuckling. His more primal side found the antics sexy as hell.

"You keep that up and I might." Shane shot Dustin a wink and arched his eyebrows.

Dustin wriggled again, his cock flopping against his crotch. "Yeah, whatever." Dustin paused and he watched Shane. "I'm hungry and wish we had strawberries. I had strawberries and chocolate once. It was damn good."

Shane was a bit shaken that Dustin had shifted from gay sex to berries. "Sorry. It's so late that everything's closed. Maybe some other time."

"Yeah, maybe."

Shane finished the last email and closed his computer. He glanced at the clock on the side of the bed and fought back a yawn. "I'm beat. I think I'll get some sleep."

Dustin grabbed Shane's shoulder and shoved him toward their bed. "Wimp! You need a big pair to hang with a bull rider."

Shane chuckled and shoved back. "Whatever, you little shit. Next time you can be on foot in the arena and we'll see how *you* do."

Dustin raked his gaze across Shane's body. "Nah, I'd rather be on the bull."

They slid into the bed, but Shane wondered what the consequences of his admission to Dustin might be.

Chapter Four

Dustin woke to a soft voice easing him to consciousness. He fought to keep the fantasy of his stiff cock buried deep in Shane's hot ass. Dustin was slamming his cock into Shane, his breath coming in powerful gasps as he neared his release.

"Dustin. Umm, Dustin."

He buried himself deep with each thrust.

"Dustin!"

He struggled to wake, confusion flooding his mind as he worked to differentiate between fantasy and reality.

"Dustin, your little guy is kinda knocking at my back door."

He stopped thrusting and brought the words into sync with the tingle coming from his groin. Reality hit him harder than a baseball bat.

He shoved himself across the bed, moving as far away as he could from Shane. "Oh fuck! Shit! Dude, I can't believe I did that. I was dreaming."

Shane gazed over his shoulder to Dustin. "It's okay. Don't sweat it. You see a hot chick then dream about her."

Dustin's heart raced. After having been thrown out of his dad's house, he could count on one hand the number of people who knew he was gay. He'd been with guys, but his hookups had been so deep in the closet that light had never entered their world.

"Shane, man, I'm so sorry. I don't know what happened."

"Calm down. It's not a big deal. Everyone has sex dreams. I was just the warm body next to you. It didn't have anything to do with me. I'm sure you were dreaming about some gorgeous cowgirl."

The panic of being discovered built in Dustin. Years of hiding part of his identity had him exhausted. His attraction to the muscular bullfighter was the final straw. *No more hiding.*

"No," said Dustin.

"Yeah. It's just something that happens. I won't say a word if that's what's worrying you." Shane waved his hand.

Dustin took a deep breath. "No, I meant it wasn't a chick. I like guys." *I like you.*

Shane snapped his gaze back on Dustin. "You mean you're gay? Since when?"

Fear and anxiety flooded Dustin as the words came to life. "Yeah, since pretty much forever, but it's not the most popular thing around here. You get it?"

"Yes, I understand. I'm the same. I don't want it all over the circuit."

"Yeah, that's cool. Sorta our secret."

Shane glanced down at his crotch and saw Dustin's rock-hard dick. Then Shane met his eyes and they shared a knowing expression.

Dustin flushed hot at the attention. Shane's scent of lust and desire made him even hornier. Shane had a slight smirk, his hands behind his head. *No way Shane wants to hook up with me. Does he feel something, too?* Dustin glanced at Shane. "You got wood, too?"

Shane turned toward Dustin, the sheet tented over his crotch. "What do you think?"

Dustin darted his gaze around the room, jumping from the clothing he'd strewn all over and to the mirror before returning to the rumpled bed, his cock doing most of the thinking. "We could fool around, right? I mean, we're both into guys and shit. I'm all horned up." He pleaded with Shane. "I promise not to narc you out."

An odd combination of desire and reservation flashed in Shane's expression but disappeared so fast that Dustin couldn't be certain.

"Sure. I'm horny, too. It's been a while."

Dustin sat on the bed, his cock jutting in front of him, and stared at Shane. "You'd put out?" A drop of pre-cum ran down the underside of Dustin's cock at the idea of having sex with Shane.

"Hey, you're good-looking and I'm all scarred. I'm not interested in a pity fuck."

"You'd let me fuck you? I just thought we'd do hand— Wait, why a pity fuck? You're hot."

Shane flipped back the sheet, his thick cock bobbing up from his crotch.

Dustin's focus snapped to Shane's dick and its surrounding thatch of curly hair. Dustin had never seen a cock that turned him on so much. He caught Shane's sharp, musky scent and realized he'd missed part of the conversation.

"The scars. I don't see how you could think I'm hot when I'm all cut up."

Dustin scooted closer and searched Shane's expression for a clue to help him interpret his words. He lifted his hand, closing the distance to the scar bisecting Shane's face. He hovered, staring into his deep blue eyes. Shane gave a nearly imperceptible nod and Dustin inched his finger to the pale welt. From the edge of Shane's hairline, Dustin followed the scar over the line through his brow until it resumed on Shane's cheek. The slight texture rubbing against Dustin's finger only heightened his desire.

God, he's hot. Doesn't he realize the scars are like badges of honor for all the cowboys he's saved?

"Dustin, what did you have in mind? It's been a while and you're cute. But I want the whole foreplay thing, including kissing." Shane nodded at Dustin's cock and the pre-cum flowing from it like a leaky faucet. "You're cute and I'm horny. But I want you to know what I want. It's not that I'm expecting a wedding proposal, but I refuse to be a rodeo quickie."

Confusion welled up in Dustin. "You want to kiss?"

Shane locked eyes with Dustin. "I love to kiss. I love foreplay. But—"

"Hey, I already told you I'm gay. My mom died when I was young and my dad and grandpa raised me," Dustin blurted out. "I was seventeen when they found me in the barn sucking the neighbor kid off and they threatened to kill me. They said there'd never been a fag in our family and there wouldn't be one now. I had to leave that night. Todd's mom and dad let me stay with them, kept me off the street. I've had a few hookups, guys I found online. But if you're up for it, I think it would be..." *Amazing? Mind-blowing? Life changing?*

Shane rolled onto his elbow. "Why didn't you tell me last night? It would've made the whole thing easier for me."

"I dunno. I just didn't think of it. I guess it was like your time and I didn't want to screw it up."

"I can see that." Shane hesitated before continuing. "Yeah, I'm good with fooling around, but it's not going to be wham-bam-thank-you thing."

Dustin's heart constricted and his body flooded with eager anticipation. "Yeah, sure. It'll be fun."

Shane rolled over and fished condoms and lube from his bag. He set them on the side table and cocked an eyebrow at Dustin. "I like to be prepared, just in case. I get lucky sometimes."

You'd get lucky all the time with me.

"Sounds good." Dustin felt like a fumbling adolescent, not a twenty-one-year-old. His body filled with waves of desire when he studied every inch of Shane as they lay side by side. Dustin knew he wouldn't last long. He trembled at the thought of being with Shane. He was so close to the edge. His awkwardness built, increasing his insecurity. The sight of Shane's broad chest made Dustin feel inadequate. He struggled to stay calm. "Umm, what do you want to do first?"

Shane ran his tongue over his lips and Dustin's heart melted. "Kissing is good — or just touching each other."

The heat of Dustin's face at the idea of caressing Shane was like he'd stood in front of a bonfire. "Can I...? Is it okay...? Some of that stuff?"

"Hey. Whatever you want, just ask."

"Can I touch your chest?"

Shane glanced at his torso. "Sure. Knock yourself out." He reclined on the pillows and put his interlaced fingers behind his head. "Go for it."

Dustin moved in, his typical bravado gone. He sat close. His cock flexed at the heat between them. A spinneret of pre-cum ran from the tip to Shane's thigh. Dustin glanced down. "Seems like the little guy is reeling you in."

Shane winked. "He already caught me."

Dustin's focus narrowed as he touched Shane's chest. When he ran his palms across Shane, each dark curly hair sent a shiver through Dustin. He pressed his face against Shane's neck and inhaled. The masculine aroma forced a small groan from him. He glanced up and lost himself in Shane's smile.

"I shaved my chest once. It itched so much that it made me miserable. So I trim it up a bit. The guys I'm with are drunk and horny. They don't care," Shane offered.

Dustin eased his fingers through the thick hair coating Shane's arm. Leaning in, he kissed the underside of Shane's thick biceps. When he raised his head, Shane had a strange expression.

"What?"

"I'm hairy, scarred and ugly as fuck, but you think I'm hot. You could have anyone you wanted. You're the poster child for a blond stud. What the hell's your deal?"

The sudden change in topic didn't phase Dustin. His entire life had been like that, so he thought nothing of it as he traced the outline of a thick scar on Shane's shoulder. "I like guys that look like guys. I like you. You're sexy." Dustin cocked an eyebrow and glared at

Shane. "And if you say you're ugly one more time, I'm gonna band you."

Shane chuckled and crossed his legs. "I'll be good. I like my balls attached."

"I thought so. Now, less talking."

Dustin moved closer until they touched. He inhaled deeply and held it as he enjoyed Shane's scent filling the air around him. He flicked his tongue out to taste Shane before running his nose along Shane's jaw then burying himself in the short, curly hair at the base of his skull. He nibbled on Shane's ear and worked his way down until the lobe slipped between his lips. Shane tilted his head to one side, his eyes easing closed as Dustin worked his magic. A small sigh escaped Shane's lips when Dustin released his earlobe.

"I haven't had a lot of experience, so if I'm doing something wrong..." Dustin said sheepishly.

Shane opened his eyes and gaped at Dustin. "You're doing great. No complaints from the ugl— From me."

"Well, I have watched a lot of porn." Dustin let out an uninhibited laugh.

"You did a damn good job on your homework, because I'm boned up."

Dustin locked eyes with Shane. "I want to kiss you."

He lifted his hand toward Dustin. "I'd like that. I'd like it a lot."

Their lips brushed, but the pulses running through Dustin made bolts of lightning seem inadequate. His cock flexed and smeared pre-cum over Shane's hairy thigh. The contact drove a trembling breath from Dustin. His balls snapped against his shaft and his dick jumped. *Fuck! Algebra. Changing oil. Mucking stalls! Fuck!* He convulsed, shooting across Shane, his cries louder with each spasm. Dustin rolled his eyes as the spicy scent of sex drifted through the air. With a final high whine, Dustin collapsed on Shane, panting.

Shane trailed a light touch across Dustin's chest. "That was hot."

"Sorry! It. Was. Too good."

When their eyes met, Dustin could see the melancholy, even as he enjoyed Shane's finger sliding along his jaw.

"Don't worry. It's fine. You got off," Shane said.

Dustin pinned the larger man onto the bed, threw his leg over and sat on Shane's groin, his hard cock trapped under Dustin.

"Come on. I need to shower so we can head out."

Dustin clamped his legs tight around Shane as he tried to unseat Dustin.

"I ride bulls and I'm damn good. You ain't bucking me off." Dustin leered at him and ran his fingers over Shane's chest. "I can go again in a few minutes. Sorry, but when my dick ran over your leg, the fireworks went off."

Shane's expression relaxed from a tight frown. "A few minutes, huh?"

Joy filled Dustin and he bounced on top of Shane. "Yup, give me a couple of minutes and the old pecker will be back in action."

Dustin's bounces gained in altitude until Shane grabbed his thighs and pinned him down. "Easy! You're smashing my balls."

Dustin grinned and lay across Shane. He wanted to focus on Shane's request as well as get a kiss. He braced his hands on either side of Shane's head and lowered himself until he sensed the heat of Shane's mouth against his own.

"You said you wanted hardcore kisses?" Dustin asked.

Shane seemed a little overwhelmed, but nodded.

Dustin moved that last bit of distance between their lips. When he made contact, Dustin thought they had been touched by a hot iron, and the heat swept through his body like a summer grassfire. The sensation was like nothing he'd experienced before and it was one he was hungry to explore in more depth. Dustin twisted his head and pressed harder as the urgency of his passion built with each kiss. He ground his body against Shane until he couldn't go any further.

Dustin stopped squirming, cocked his head and considered Shane. "Do you like having your nipples messed with?"

Rather than answer, Shane smirked and flicked his fingers against his hard nubs. A deep groan filled the room as Shane enjoyed the sensation. "Yeah, it's fucking hot to have them played with," Shane said.

Dustin leaned over, caressing Shane's sides. He let his thumbs touch the stiff tips. Shane sank back against the bed as his eyes fluttered closed. Dustin pressed his body against Shane's, reached out with his tongue and flicked around the quarter-size circle.

"Yeah, that's good."

Dustin licked over Shane's nipples — first one, then the other. Shane caressed his back, leaving trails of warmth over him. He lifted himself from Shane and traced his finger along the scar again. "I love to touch you. And what do you know, little Dustin is waking up!" Dustin lifted his hips. His plump cock expanded from its trapped position between them and slid into place beside Shane's dick.

"Glad to hear it. He seems like a world of fun."

Dustin slid down, intent on Shane's crotch. Shane lifted himself to his elbows as Dustin studied his package. He met Shane's gaze with a guarded expression. "Sorry, but you're bigger than I am. And you have a curve."

"Yeah, well, that's the equipment I got in the deal. Sorry if it isn't what you expected…"

Without another word, Dustin sank his mouth over the thick head and eased lower, sliding deeper inch by inch until his lips pressed against Shane's pubic hair.

"Holy shit!" Shane yelled.

Dustin lifted his head until his mouth popped off Shane's dick. "You're a perfect fit."

"Damn! You told me you didn't know how to do stuff."

"I've never shoved the whole thing down before. But I thought yours would fit, and it did."

"You're crazy."

Rather than reply, Dustin did a repeat performance. Shane's thick cock slid down his throat as he drove forward. The head compressed as he swallowed while his body relaxed and accepted the intruder. His world narrowed to the pleasure of moving up and down the length of Shane's shaft several delicious times. Shane tugged at him and Dustin let it slide free.

"Something wrong?"

Shane struggled for control, his face red and sweat-covered. "You gotta stop if you want to fuck—or I'm gonna come."

"I'm hard again…"

Shane grabbed a condom, tore it open then wrapped his fingers around Dustin's dick and unrolled the condom.

"See? It's smaller than yours."

"You know, most guys wouldn't say they're smaller."

Dustin shrugged. "It's a dick. And like you said, it's what I got. No one's ever complained."

Shane considered Dustin, then rolled over.

"Why did you do that?" Dustin asked.

Shane glanced over his shoulder. "Do what?"

"Roll onto your stomach. I can't see your face if you do that."

"Well—most guys don't want to see my face when we're screwing."

Without a word, Dustin grabbed Shane then flipped him over. After squeezing his rock-hard dick, Dustin grabbed Shane's balls and stretched them tight. "I told you I'd band you next time that rolled outta your mouth."

"Hey! Easy. I was just answering you! Don't rip my balls off."

Dustin let them slip from his hand then picked up the lube and squirted it down the length of his cock, covering it with a thick coat. He lifted Shane's legs and moved closer.

"Hey, how about some on me, too? I'm not a virgin, but it's been a while."

"Oh. Okay." Dustin picked up the tube again and squirted some on his fingers. He slid his hand between Shane's legs and smeared the gel over his hole. As he pressed his finger against its tight entrance, Shane tensed, forcing Dustin to press harder until his finger slipped inside. Shane trembled under Dustin's touch.

"I need my dick inside you. I'm horny as fuck again," said Dustin.

He slid his hands up the back of Shane's thighs and pressed them toward his chest. Dustin's cock bounced in front of him as they moved closer. He met Shane's gaze. "Ready?"

"Yeah, just kinda take it—"

Dustin slammed inside Shane. Once he hit bottom, he froze in place, luxuriating in the tight heat.

"Fuck!" Shane's face shot crimson and a fine sheen of sweat appeared on his body. "Damn, Dustin! Slow down next time. Don't just shove it in."

"Sorry. I'll take it out."

"No! I mean no, wait a minute. It's already better." Shane lifted his torso and grimaced. "Good thing you're not bigger."

They spent several minutes caressing each other while Shane recovered. Dustin shivered at Shane's touch across his nipple.

With a deep sigh, Shane relaxed. "Try again, but start slow," Shane said.

Dustin pulled back and searched Shane's face for signs of pain. The ring of Shane's ass constricted around his cock. A groan drifted to Dustin's ears as he pressed back inside. Soon he was ramming in and out at a steady pace, his climax building. *Hold off. For God's sake, hold off this time.*

"Harder," came the urgent demand from Shane.

Dustin clenched his ass and drove his steel-hard cock into Shane. He grabbed Shane's ankles, bent him in half and pounded his butt. He delayed his orgasm this time. He crawled on top and braced his feet against the mattress with Shane curled under him. A little later Shane's body shook. Dustin slowed, concerned he might have injured him.

"You okay?"

"Oh, hell yes! You found my sweet spot. Don't stop now."

Dustin pushed Shane's legs higher. He arched his body and slammed into the bullfighter. Shane grabbed his cock and stroked fast and hard while Dustin pounded him. The frequent whimpers and yelps spurred Dustin to fuck harder, lost in the intensity of his passion. He curled closer, kissing Shane as he fucked him with no mercy.

A hot brand seared across Dustin's chest when Shane erupted. Shane's cock tensed and a second jet of white shot from its tip. This time the trail ended on Dustin's lips. He licked them and a bittersweet flavor flowed through his body like lava and left him tingling. Overwhelmed, Dustin bucked into Shane like a stallion breeding his mare. They merged and separated. Shane's groin had tightened with orgasm. The smell of sex surrounded them.

Dustin climaxed as Shane's orgasm receded. They writhed over each other with sweaty bodies as Dustin's pleasure crested and crashed down on him. When the tingle faded and the last drops oozed into the condom, he collapsed onto Shane, gasping for air. Shane ran his hands over Dustin's back, sending waves of desire through him.

"Unless you want another round, you best stop," Dustin warned.

Shane let out a barely audible laugh and settled his hands. He lifted his head and met Shane's deep blue eyes. He caressed Shane's face before leaning close for another kiss. Their touch lingered and the warmth of their time together flowed through Dustin. He locked his gaze with Shane. "You're so fucking hot."

Shane's face fell, and he turned away from Dustin. "Come on. Get off me. I need a shower."

Shane's shift in moods left Dustin confused. "What's wrong? Did I do something?"

Shane sighed and gave Dustin a sad smile that left Dustin feeling he'd missed something. "You didn't do anything. We need to be in Cody this afternoon so we need to head out."

Dustin kept the sense of awkwardness he couldn't seem to shake. "You sure? It seems like —"

Shane kissed him and rubbed his hand over Dustin's smooth face. "Everything's fine. The sex was fantastic. Relax."

Dustin's focus shattered. He vaulted to his feet, grabbed Shane's arm and helped him up. "Come on! We can shower together. It'll be a blast."

* * * *

Shane dried himself. Even this second hot shower hadn't erased all the aches from his time in the arena the previous day. His butt tingled. *Damn, I'm glad he isn't any bigger than he is or the eight-hour drive ahead of me would be miserable. Nothing like sitting on a ripped ass to make a drive unpleasant.*

Dustin bounced in front of the tiny motel room sink to some kind of internal rhythm. He set an orange prescription bottle on the counter along with his toothbrush and other stuff. The towel clung to Dustin's wiggling hips by magic for several seconds, then dropped to the floor.

He has a cute bubble butt. It's made for fucking.

Dustin reached down, grabbed the towel and tossed it over his shoulder. Shane enjoyed the show the young bull rider delivered while he finished drying his good bits.

Dustin's motions contained a certain frantic energy. He opened the bottle, fished out a single pill and washed it down with a drink of water. Their eyes met in the mirror and Dustin shrugged.

"Adderall, for my ADHD. I've been taking something since first grade." He let out a snort. "Maybe if I'd been taking it the day Granddad caught me sucking Steven, I would have realized his normal time to get home might not have been the best time to be fooling around."

Shane considered Dustin's revelation while the younger man finished his morning routine. Knowing they were about to spend hours together in his pickup, Shane hoped the trip with Dustin didn't become something else he'd regret. Although their early morning sex had been good enough that Shane was willing to tolerate a few hours with someone who acted like a monkey on speed.

After leaving their hotel, Shane made good time toward their destination. Dustin made the trip even easier by going to sleep curled against the door. That gave Shane the opportunity to enjoy a quiet drive through southern Wyoming. When they'd started out in the early morning, Dustin had been a constant source of chatter, nothing bad. He'd talked a lot about the relationship he had with Todd, similar to what he and Sam shared. But the constant dialog had worn on Shane by the time Dustin had fallen asleep. But a snort from the figure curled against the door signaled Dustin's return to the world of the conscious and the end of Shane's quiet travels. He uncoiled his arms and growled out a yawn.

"Damn, where are we?" Dustin asked.

"Somewhere in southern Wyoming. A few more hours and we'll make Cody."

Dustin squirmed in the seat, grabbed his crotch and clamped down. "Man, I gotta piss really bad."

Shane glanced back in the rearview mirror and found the flat expanse of state highway deserted. Without comment, he eased the pickup to the side of the road. The truck was still rolling forward when Dustin escaped from his seatbelt and vaulted to the ground.

Shane turned off the ignition, his eyes on the horizon, ready to resume their trip. After he scanned the road several more times, he realized Dustin was still peeing. He reached back and opened the pickup's rear window. "What's taking you so long? You aren't jacking off, are you?"

Dustin snorted, shaking his arm as he finished. "Nah, just writing my name in the gravel."

Oh crap, is he twelve?

Dustin jumped back into the pickup cab and Shane drove onto the highway. After a few miles, he realized Dustin was still groping himself. "What's up? You know that thing has a shelf life."

"I'm kinda horny. Maybe I'll bring him out, give him some air and see what happens."

"How can you be horny? You got off twice this morning." Shane stared at him, drifting toward the side of the road as he lost focus on what he was doing.

"Dude, I'm always horny. It's like I can never get off enough."

Shane's humor built with each passing second. A puzzled expression covered Dustin's face. "What?"

"Guys your age are supposed to be horny, but you might be an overachiever."

Dustin smirked at Shane. "No big deal. I just thought it might be fun to get off while we're traveling. You know, road head. Like, it'd be a rush."

Shane glanced from the road to find Dustin with his hand down the front of his jeans. "Me driving down the highway with you sucking me off would be a terrible idea. What would I say if we get stopped? 'Sorry, dude. My friend thought it would be a cool idea to suck my dick while I was doing eighty down the interstate'."

"Whatever," Dustin said.

Over the next few miles Dustin slipped his hand out but kept his gaze on the unending miles of grass with a sprinkling of cattle. As they sped closer to Cody, a tense silence developed between the two of them. Without a glance at Shane, Dustin muttered, "I'm not stupid. Just 'cause I'm hyper doesn't mean I'm a dumb bull rider. I take my meds, but it's not like there's a cure. It's kinda like being gay."

"I never said you were dumb," Shane said.

"Just now you gave me the same stare as everyone else. Like because I wanna have fun and loosen up then I'm stupid. Everyone does it. I guess I'd hoped you might be different."

"Sorry. I didn't intend to do that to you. I know what it's like to have people not understand."

The scenery maintained its monotony as they sat in contemplative silence.

"I get on your nerves, too. Don't I?"

Shane glanced at the man beside him. *What's going on here? Why is the biggest cut-up on the circuit suddenly getting all thoughtful on me?*

"I don't know. Why? Does it matter? It's not like you'll want to hang out."

Dustin's brows furrowed. "Why not?"

"Because you're a hot shit. Hot shits don't hang with me. Second, I'm a rodeo clown who's hoping to get enough votes to make National Finals and you're a bull rider who is almost certain to make it. And last, you aren't out even as much as I am, which isn't much."

Dustin locked his gaze on Shane. "You think I wouldn't want to hang out with you?"

"I'm twenty-six and some days I look and feel forty. I'm just the latest guy who has agreed to sleep with you. I have enough scars to chase off anyone. I'm sure you're not searching for another problem. A boyfriend would sure be a huge new one."

"You really don't get it, do you?" Dustin stared into the distance, refusing to meet Shane's gaze.

"Get what?"

Dustin didn't answer. The silence continued as Dustin's eyes locked on the passing vista, then they eased shut.

Shane glanced at Dustin, his gut a whirlwind of emotions. *Why is he fighting me so hard when I'm trying to give him an easy out? What the fuck is happening?*

Chapter Five

Shane paced outside the gate, eager to check on Dustin. He'd just finished his ride and taken a nasty fall. Their conversation on the way to Cody still haunted Shane. That Dustin viewed his scarred body with anything but apprehension baffled him. He hated to admit it, but the hyperactive youngster and his crazy antics tugged on Shane's heartstrings in a way he hadn't experienced before. Nothing was going to come of it. Dustin was far out of his league. Their shared intimacy wouldn't happen again. Dustin would dump him like the others had. Shane couldn't see any other resolution. The veneer of concern coming from Dustin had created a shred of hope in Shane, which meant Dustin dumping him would be painful.

He spotted Dustin leaving the arena in an animated conversation with Todd, the friend Shane had met at the bar. *I thought the bull rider left for a different rodeo. Guess his plans changed at the last moment.* Dustin flailed about, his arms adding emphasis to whatever he was saying, the long fringe on his chaps swinging with each step as his boots kicked up tiny whirls of dust.

Shane thought he caught a happy glint when their eyes met.

"Damn bull tried to jack with me," Dustin said.

Todd, oblivious to the interaction, continued to goad Dustin. "Just admit it. I'm better than you are. I'll whip your ass at Nationals."

"Fuck you, Todd."

As they walked past, Dustin gave Shane a small wave. Shane trotted to catch up then matched their enthusiastic pace. "Hey, if you'd like, I can make sure everything's okay. I'm an EMT."

Dustin turned his head toward Shane and winked. "It's no big deal, man. Just another goose egg on my hard skull."

"Yeah, his hard head's been banged plenty of times." Todd popped Dustin on the arm and dashed out of reach. "He's been hit so many times that he forgets to dodge now."

Dustin and Todd degenerated into adolescent horseplay for a few steps. The two tripped and shoved each other while they kept up the banter. Shane understood now it was their way of showing affection.

"Yeah, whatever… I dodge fine. You're the one who's eatin' dirt at every arena you've ridden in since you were fourteen." He mimed eating from a bowl then wagged his eyebrows at Todd.

"Whatever, Lewis. Just remember who has more notches on his headboard." Before the banter continued, Todd glanced at his watch and started toward an exit. "Hey, I gotta get ready for my ride. You going with me to Colorado Springs?"

"Yeah. Don't fuck up and forget me."

Todd spun on his heel, shot Dustin a grin and flipped him off before disappearing through the exit.

Dustin shook his head. "He's a good guy. He'd do anything for me. It's like we're brothers. I don't know what would have happened if his folks hadn't let me stay with 'em." Dustin stared at Shane. "We need to talk. About... You know."

Shane saw where this was going — another morning-after speech. But it wouldn't be him being dumped this time. Maybe the refusal to be hurt was Dustin's fault. He shouldn't have treated Shane like an actual living, breathing person. His honest kindness and irreverent behavior were only a few of the traits Shane had grown to like about Dustin. Most of his hookups were glad enough for a piece of ass but didn't want any emotional attachment.

All his positive attributes would make the inevitable end of this conversation even more painful than usual. Determined to count first coupe, Shane began, "Hey, it's great that you didn't get messed up out there. It seemed nasty. I guess we'll see each other...whenever."

Dustin swallowed several times in rapid succession, his Adam's apple bouncing up and down like a super ball and tears forming in the corners of his eyes.

What the hell? The others had either disappeared or seemed relieved when he'd given them an excuse to leave and not worry that he would out them. When Dustin stood without moving, Shane turned to leave.

Dustin grabbed his arm. "Last night was fun. Mind-blowing, actually. I get that you disagree, but you're hot."

He spun and disappeared into the crowd, leaving Shane gaping after him.

Fuck. What's that supposed to mean? If it was important to him, he should have stayed to talk. Shane stood in a stupor until he realized Todd had reappeared.

"Hey," Todd said.

Shane fought to bring his jumbled thoughts together. "Hey, sorry. I was spacing."

"Yeah, I caught that." Todd dusted off his hands on his jeans before meeting Shane's gaze. "Seen Dustin?"

"He headed out that way." Shane nodded toward the pens.

"I need to find the little shit."

"He needs someone to watch out for him. He's a loose cannon," Shane said.

"Don't count him out too soon. Dustin had more goals in high school than I have now. He's a stand-up guy. He'd go down helping a friend."

"Oh, I understand. He's part of the bull riders' fraternity. You guys stick together."

"No, man, not like Dustin. One time we were in this bar in Houston and a bunch of guys jumped me. Dustin flew into them like a buzz saw. They'd have beaten the crap outta me before I got loose if it weren't for him."

Shane studied the bull rider for several seconds. "That doesn't sound like the guy I met. He's like a hyper kid."

Todd nodded. "Oh yeah, he can be a wild son of a bitch. He's always been there for me, though."

"Didn't he live with you?"

"Still does. Well, as much as anywhere. My parents, brothers and sisters all love him like one of the family." Todd paused, considered Shane and lifted one eyebrow. "If anyone were to hurt him, I'd kick their ass to Canada and back." The gaze stayed trained on Shane until he squirmed. "Know what I mean?" Todd asked.

Shane tilted his head at Todd, giving him a quirky smile. "Yeah, I hear ya."

Todd nodded and relaxed. "Think Diablo will end up being in the finals?"

Shane snorted. "You mean the top-ranked bull on the circuit? Yeah, I'd bet he will."

"Damn it. That bastard is nothing but evil. Needs a bullet between his eyes."

Shane trailed his fingers over his face. "Something like that…"

* * * *

Dustin sat on the hard boards that formed the seating for the small outdoor arena. He'd been searching for something to break up his afternoon. He was still struggling with his feelings about Shane, as if it made a damn bit of difference what he thought. Shane seemed determined to make it clear that he didn't want to spend any time with him, regardless of what was said. But one of the other bull riders had suggested he watch the peewee rodeo going on.

Dustin had done the peewee circuit when he'd been younger and had pleasant memories of the friendly competition. Once he'd decided on his destination, it took longer for him to find the small outdoor arena where the kids were competing.

The heat of the brilliant afternoon sun created a shimmer rising from the bleachers. The high school's and kids' rodeos were always in the afternoon. It didn't draw the crowds like the pro rodeo did each evening. The chance of someone getting hurt always drew the most attendance.

The people watching this competition were mostly parents and friends, but some of the best action happened during the afternoon rodeo. It didn't hurt that it also had the funniest moments. It hadn't been too long ago since he'd been one of the group in the arena baking in the afternoon sun. But today all he wanted was a place to think. The surrounding activity helped Dustin concentrate, unlike how it would affect most people, making this the perfect place.

Dustin realized they were about to begin the sheep riding. For Dustin, this was one of the funniest events in rodeo. There wasn't much bucking or snorting. Truth be told, there wasn't any — just a kid in a helmet and pads, a double handful of wool and a dead run across the arena. Dustin laughed when the little guy who'd drawn the biggest sheep went airborne when the sheep froze, throwing the kid over its head.

Dustin had made innumerable similar rides in the days when his mother had still been alive and his father and grandfather had still acknowledged him. Now Todd and his family were all he had, no different from what it had been for the last handful of years. Shane had appeared, but he didn't seem to want him — or at least not like Dustin hoped. Making out in the motel room had been the hottest thing Dustin had ever experienced. None of the other handful of times he'd had sex had come close. There had been an emotional connection he'd never had before. That Shane was sexy, too, didn't hurt.

Dustin didn't understand why Shane wanted to push him away. No, he understood. It was the same reason as always. He wore on people's nerves. He chattered too much, demanded too much, *was* too much.

His attention was drawn back to the arena when a barrel racer jumped across the start and pounded toward the first of the three drums. Dustin grinned at how the girl's blonde hair matched the coat of her Palomino. He was sure the match wasn't by accident. She made her turn too sharp and knocked a barrel over. *Well, that sucks.*

The next contestant was a tiny girl on a huge black horse. The diminutive girl's legs stuck out at right angles from the saddle. Even from where Dustin sat, he could see the blood-red lining of the horse's nose as it flared its nostrils. The animal was excited and eager to go. Dustin wondered if it was a hot-blooded horse, one that loved the competition—or both. A few minutes from now and he'd know.

The buzzer sounded and the horse and girl merged into a single being. She pressed herself onto its neck as it pounded for the first barrel. Dustin considered barrel racing about as interesting as golf, but this run held him riveted. She guided her horse with invisible touches as it flew through the pattern. With the final turn, she clung to his back like a tick for the flying trip to the finish line. Dustin found himself jumping to his feet to cheer her on, along with the rest of the crowd. When she crossed the line, Dustin held his breath for the time to be announced. *Fifteen seconds. Damn good for this arena. I bet she isn't even twelve.*

Dustin sat down, his attention diverted from the reason he'd come. He admired the rider. She had guts. Dustin let out a sigh. *Not like me. I hide behind everything and anyone. A cocky attitude keeps most people at a distance. I've never even told Todd and he's my best friend. I keep chickening out.*

Dustin was drawn back into the action in the arena when the girl who'd ridden so well during the barrel race charged out of the gate on the same massive horse for the goat tying. Luck wasn't with her this time. She'd drawn a goat that outweighed her, and she wasn't large enough to throw the animal. Obviously knowing the girl couldn't finish otherwise, a ringman ran over and flipped the goat for her. She was disqualified, but his action allowed her to finish her run. *Not her fault. You can't be something you ain't.*

Dustin considered his personal demons again. He wasn't going to be something he wasn't, either. He was gay. That fact wouldn't change. His family's opinion hadn't mattered for years. Dustin was surprised. He'd known this for a long time. *Why did it take a little girl with a huge amount of grit to show me? What about Shane? Where does he fit into this whole unraveling mess?*

"And now, the bullfighter for this afternoon, Shane Rees."

The announcement jarred Dustin but he scanned the ring and spotted Shane working the crowd. Shane didn't do elaborate entertainment like the guys hired to be clowns, but he'd get at least a few laughs. Dustin sat motionless and watched the man who had stirred up the emotions he'd buried at seventeen. A few minutes later, the first rider shot out of the chute on a small bull with no horns. Dustin could have dismissed the easy ride, but he understood that for the contestant it was every bit as important as conquering Diablo was to him. He rode his eight seconds and had done a decent job, in Dustin's opinion, but his dismount didn't go well and he landed flat on his back, stunned. The bull turned back, probably not out of malice but fear, and ran toward the rider. Shane appeared from nowhere, startled him away at the last second, then helped the kid off the ground.

"What a sweet boy."

Dustin twisted to find a woman had seated herself beside him while he had been glued to the arena. "Yes, ma'am. That your grandson?"

"Oh heavens, no. I was talking about the clown. He's such a nice young man. He volunteers to help with the kids' rodeo every year."

"Volunteers?"

"Sure. The kids' rodeo is all run by volunteers. This is the fifth year the Rees boy has been our rodeo clown."

Dustin stopped paying attention to the woman talking to him as he watched Shane playing a game of tag with a second bull. *He volunteers. For free. To help.*

Dustin sat for a long time, ignoring additional comments from his neighbor and considered this strange man who had entered his life. This was a new facet of Shane that he hadn't known before, and the revelation changed the situation for Dustin again. He needed to get questions answered and soon.

Once the junior rodeo ended, Dustin wandered through the fairgrounds and enjoyed a few of the rides. Most of them were tame measured against his need for adrenaline but they were still fun. After a few enjoyable hours had passed, he realized he needed to dress for the evening. Once he had everything in place, he made his way to the arena to watch the rounds ahead of him.

As he took in the competitors, Dustin propped his leg on the fencing and adjusted the buckles on his chaps until they were a perfect fit. He checked off each item in a routine he'd begun almost half his life ago. His only change from his earlier years was that he'd ditched the protective vest and helmet. When he wore them, he had more trouble reading the bull. Besides, he was a lone wolf, anyway. One day the pack would take him down.

"Are you kidding me? Still being the biggest dumbass in the West?"

Dustin glanced back at the source of the familiar voice and smiled. "Yeah, right. I can't be the dumbass of the West. That's your title. But are you bitching at me about not wearing the protective junk? I've told you before that shit makes it harder to ride."

Todd scowled at Dustin. "Not wearing the gear is going to get you messed up in a bad way. Now, are you going to help me check that I have everything on right and I didn't miss anything?"

Todd released a sigh and glared at him.

It took all Dustin's willpower not to retort. But he waited as his friend stepped around and checked Dustin's work. It took only a few minutes before Todd patted the last buckle in place.

But Todd wasn't ready to give in to Dustin's decision. "Come on! Your damn skull is thick, but—"

Dustin grabbed his arm, tugged Todd into a chest bump then released him. After a couple of seconds, Dustin shook his head. "Shut up."

With that, Dustin turned and left. His focus had shifted to the bull he would ride in a few minutes. He stood on the bottom of the fence, studying the riders ahead of him as they were tossed by their bulls before they reached the end of their eight seconds.

Dustin mentally rode each bull along with the cowboy doing the actual ride. He visualized each go as if it were his. He was aware of some of the strange glances he got, but he had moved past caring about other people's opinions—well, mostly.

He was toward the end of the round so he shifted his focus back to going through his own ride — except for a few times when a bull did a move Dustin hadn't experienced before. But the time finally came for Dustin to climb on his draw. From this point onward, Dustin was running on autopilot.

The bull fought the chute as Dustin climbed over his eight-second mount. It paused for long enough to let him settle into place. The time had arrived and Dustin gave a sharp nod.

His signal released the gate on the compact dark-red assassin whose ton of muscle was a match for Dustin's determination. The bull made a jump and just missed the edge of the gate as he entered his first spin, but it was far from the first time Dustin had experienced this maneuver. He made the needed adjustments to allow him to stay centered on the bull's back.

After a final vicious spin, the bull changed direction and uncoiled a whole new level of destruction. But Dustin countered each snap of muscle and sinew without seeming to need to do anything more than react. His muscles tightened and eased in response to the bull's wild ride.

Dustin's instincts came alive as he approached the final seconds. He spurred for all he was worth, trying to increase his point earnings. The bull planted his front feet and began flipping end for end, but Dustin deflected every move.

As the final second appeared on the arena clock, the bull doubled down and sunfished. The whip of the maneuver pulled Dustin in tight — close enough for him to sense the breeze from the animal's horn. As it arched its back, Dustin's hat flew into the gates.

The buzzer sounded, its announcement echoing. He waited for the top of the next jump and launched himself into the air. A heartbeat later he landed on the arena floor, his arms flung high in triumph.

He turned and spotted Todd leaning over the fence, holding his hat. Dustin grinned as he trotted over, took the hat and wedged it back on his head.

"What'd you think? Pretty kick-ass, right?" Dustin said.

Todd flipped the hat from Dustin's head, turned it over and stuck his finger through a rip. He gave Dustin a sad smile.

"One more inch..."

Chapter Six

Shane turned from the county road to the familiar driveway of the ranch his family had owned for more than a century. With the rattle of admission, he drove over the wide cattle guard marking the ranch entrance. Recent returns home had been a tense combination of resignation and denial. His parents hadn't jumped up and down with joy at the news of Shane's coming out, but they at least had reacted better than Dustin's family.

It could be worse. At least I can still come home to visit.

With only a few days between rodeos, Shane hoped a trip back to the home place would help him reach some kind of equilibrium regarding how Dustin fit into all this. The house sat as a stark island of green in a sea of Texas shortgrass. Their ranch existed in the part of the high plains where stands of green marked houses and big trees were indications of the scattered original homesteads. He eased his pickup down the long driveway, checking the cattle grazing around him as the sun sank below the horizon, taking the temperature from fucking hot to oh-my-God hot.

He felt proud of the ranch as he drove through the herd of his father's pride-and-joy Beefmaster cattle. The brindle-and-yellow animals filled the pastures and no one would consider them pretty. But they were one of the few breeds able to deal with the climate of the high plains.

For Shane, the interest went beyond his father's concern for producing calves. Shane viewed them in terms of what made a star bucking bull on the rodeo circuit—horns, hooves and ferocity. Rodeo stock contractors would pay through the nose for a bull most people would take to the sale barn the first time it ran them out of a pasture or attacked a pickup. There were always one or two dangerous animals in the family herd. Shane's interest in the rogue animals was odd for most people, but his long-term plan was to raise and sell rodeo stock. Shane counted on bucking stock to be a lucrative market and a decent living for himself and his husband. *If I find a husband. I don't even have a boyfriend and I've likely ruined any chance of Dustin filling that role.*

The pickup rolled the final few feet and came to a stop in front of his parents' austere white house with its meticulously groomed lawn. Shane studied it in appreciation. His family always subscribed to beating nature into submission. His parents were up at dawn at least once a week to keep their yard within their idea of trimmed grass. As he stepped from his pickup, two streaks raced out of the barn. The dogs almost bowled him over in their enthusiasm. As he gave in to their demands for affection, Shane kneeled on the ground and petted both of them. They took full advantage and jumped over and on him, their noses crammed into every nook and cranny of his body and their tongues bathing his face with dog kisses.

"Mutt! Jeff! Get off him."

Shane smiled when he recognized his rescuer as his baby sister, Sara. He leaped to his feet and grabbed her in a tight hug. "I've missed you, sis."

"I've missed you, too. Why are you home? You didn't tell me you were coming back."

"I needed a few days to recuperate, so I decided to visit home and see your shining face. You need to get your barrel racing perfected so we can travel together. Then you'd be around all the time."

"Yeah, like Dad's ever gonna spring for a decent horse for me. That ain't happening."

"You could get a job."

"And you could eat shit."

Shane stared disapprovingly. "My, what a potty mouth you've got. You better not let Mom hear you or she'll tan your hide."

Sara dropped her gaze to the ground. "Sorry. I get frustrated. I want out of the middle-of-nowhere Texas so bad."

"Soon enough you'll be off to college and won't think about us again."

She lifted an eyebrow. "What happened to my barrel racing championship?"

He patted his sister on the shoulder. "Okay, well, here's the way it goes down. First you go to college on a rodeo scholarship, then you win National Finals."

She nudged Shane's ribs. "And has my big brother been picked as a bullfighter yet?"

He considered Sara. *I need to be careful what I tell her. It seems she's listening.* "No, it hasn't been decided yet. It's only July."

Sara leaned toward Shane and winked. "How's your love life?"

Embarrassment and doubt flooded Shane's body as he recalled the constant drift of his thoughts back to Dustin. Trying to avoid her question, he frowned. "Sara! You're only thirteen, and you do not need to be asking your big brother about—well, about that kinda stuff."

Sara chuckled and patted her brother's cheek. "You're so cute. Come on. I'm sure Mom has been watching us the whole time."

They started toward the house and, as if on cue, the rest of the family appeared on the porch. His mother stood in front, a faint smile on her lips as she wiped her hands on the floral-print apron she wore.

His dad was easier to read. The smile on his face welcomed his son home. He'd been good through the process of Shane's coming out. Matt Rees was fiercely protective of his children, and it was Shane's good fortune that the acceptance extended to his gay son.

It had been a relief to see that his brother Sam was visiting their parents. He spent his days working on the ranch, so it wasn't unusual for him to be there, but he and his wife lived a few miles away. They greeted each other with a grin and a wink. *Good signs.*

Their mother gave Shane's arm a tight squeeze. When she released it, her smile had gained a welcoming warmth. "Come give your mother a hug, then you can tell us why we are getting such a pleasant surprise."

Shane gave her a warm embrace before sharing a back-thumping welcome with Sam and their dad.

Shane followed his parents into the house. His mother motioned him to a seat in the living room. "Sit down. We have a few minutes to catch up."

Sam grabbed Shane and dragged him in for a chest bump. "I gotta go. Angie will hurt me if I'm late getting home again."

Shane sensed there was more to Sam's retreat than what was being said. But he had enough drama for the immediate future and let it go for another day.

With his brother gone and his sister outside, Shane felt outnumbered and out-maneuvered by his parents. He wanted to let them in. He wouldn't mind some love advice. He'd come home with the hope that on this trip he'd share more of his life with his family.

"What's wrong, son? What brings you home?" his mother asked.

Shane met her eyes, then the questioning gaze of his dad. *I need for them to realize.* Shane took a deep breath, trying to steel himself. *I can't do this. At twenty-six I'm still not ready to be their son — their gay son.*

"I had time and decided I'd take a short break."

"Well, we're glad to have you. Come in. Supper is almost ready. It's like I knew you were coming. I made your favorite."

Shane couldn't help but relax at the platter of chicken-fried steak filling the center of the table flanked by the big bowl of cream gravy. *Sometimes visiting home is a good thing.*

Shane decided early the next morning to do something he enjoyed. He saddled his favorite horse and took a ride across their extensive ranch. Shane didn't have a specific purpose in his search, only some time alone. He was disappointed with himself. He was too chicken to tell his parents about Dustin. This time he had no one other than himself to blame. He expected a mushroom cloud over West Texas from the reaction to his announcement of a boyfriend, but he didn't have the bravery to have that discussion.

Shane's ambling ride across the ranch eventually took him to its highest point. He slowed his mount to a walk as they neared the top. The lanky quarter horse grew restless, eager to stretch his legs and run after the leisurely pace Shane had dictated for the last hour. From this vantage point, Shane could see for miles. The flat terrain and low humidity created a crystal-clear panorama that stretched to the edge of the world.

He sighed as he dismounted and ran his hand over his animal's chestnut coat. "Take it easy, Dudley. I need a few minutes to relax. You know how Mom and Dad are." The gelding turned toward Shane and nickered before lowering his head to graze on the sparse vegetation. Shane looped the reins around the saddle horn and dismounted, knowing the well-trained animal wouldn't wander far. Shane walked the handful of yards to the crest of the hill.

In the distance lay the ranch headquarters, a speck on the horizon. There had been a time Shane had found comfort when he'd been home. But since his revelation, the sense of peace had been missing.

"Dudley, you think the family will ever accept that I'm gay? Other people have it worse. What if they'd thrown me out like Dustin's family did? I guess they are doing okay with my sexual orientation. But I don't see them expanding their acceptance to a boyfriend or husband. I'm not even sure which would have been worse in their eyes."

When Shane glanced back, the horse shook its head and snorted. "Yeah, you're right. At least I still have my balls, so I shouldn't complain, huh?"

He turned back to the tableau, his shoulders slumped and his mouth twisted. "Can you imagine if I brought Dustin home? Whatever might happen, I can almost guarantee it wouldn't be good. I guess we'll avoid talking about it until they die. They never ask about personal stuff, and I never mention it, either. But it's not like there's ever anything to tell 'em. Well, except now there is the drama with Dustin. But that doesn't seem to be more than a one-time thing."

Shane paused for a minute as he considered. "Yeah, Dudley, I got it. I don't understand my attraction to Dustin. I guess that's part of the reason I came back for a few days. I needed to be home to think it through."

As he studied the terrain surrounding him, he spotted a distant figure moving closer. Someone had been sent to retrieve him. With him home, it was prime time for his mother to call in the family for a head count. It always struck Shane as odd, because she didn't want the company. She would prefer to sit in the living room with the latest Christian romance novel while the rest of the family found ways of entertaining themselves. The only redeeming thing about the gatherings was that no one in his family ever said a word about the scars Shane found so objectionable.

As the dot moved closer, Shane realized there were two riders, not just one. "Well, crap."

Two riders meant a talk. With a sigh, he walked back and gathered the horse's reins, laughing when Dudley blew his hot breath over Shane's face. "Yeah, I feel the same way. I wonder which talk this one will be. How it's a sin or that I need the right girl." Shane grimaced.

"My last date was in high school. Poor girl wanted to go parking, and she scared me so bad that I took her home."

He swung his leg over the saddle and settled into the seat with practiced ease. He tapped his heels against the horse's flanks and they started toward the oncoming pair. Shane was too tired of the whole dance to even worry. "I might as well meet them halfway. Maybe that will shorten the whole thing."

Shane slowed to a walk as they entered the scant shade of a cottonwood grove. His horse dropped its head and slurped the cool water from the small spring originating a few feet up the hillside. He glanced over his shoulder to see his dad and Sam dismount and walk their horses to join Dudley. It surprised Shane to discover that his dad was one of the pair. He usually avoided the family 'talks'. Sam's presence was even more unusual. His twin had known Shane was gay since puberty and it hadn't ever been an issue for him.

They stood silently while the horses drank, the tension building to an uncomfortable level. Shane turned toward them, ready for the discussion to be over. "So what've I done to offend you guys?"

Shane's father jerked in obvious surprise at the question. "No one's offended. Why would you think that?"

"Dad, you and Sam came hunting for me. Anytime Mom sends two of you, it's a serious talk."

"He has you there, Dad." Sam nodded. Only a few minutes separated them and Shane was the elder, but his twin treated Shane like he was his senior — and by years and not minutes. They'd always been close. *What's going on? Sam couldn't care less that I'm gay. Why did they come to find me?*

Their dad lifted his cowboy hat and ran his fingers through his short white hair. He dug the toe of his boot in the dust a couple of times and settled the hat on the back of his head. "I guess he does." He paused and caught Shane's gaze. "I'm here for moral support. Sam needs to talk with you."

Surprised and a bit worried, Shane turned to his brother and cocked an eyebrow. "Oh? What in the world could you not talk to me about without backup? We share everything."

Sam scuffed his boots, kicking the dust as he shifted from one foot to the other, obviously working up his courage to talk to Shane about something. "Yeah..."

"Okay, well, what is it?"

"Well, Angie and I've been trying to get pregnant for a few years."

"Yes..." Confusion filled Shane as he glanced from his brother to his dad. This wasn't new information.

There was a pained expression on Sam's face when he glanced up. He turned away, his shoulders hunched in dejection. "We've been going to the fertility doctor. He says we can't have kids."

"Oh, Sam. I'm so sorry." Shane started forward to comfort his sibling but was halted by a barely perceptible shake of their father's head.

Sam sucked in air, and Shane saw he was close to tears. "And it's me. I'm shooting blanks."

Shane started to talk but remained silent, unable to think of a suitable reply. The quiet grew, expanding until the tension engulfed them all. The strain had become palpable. "I'm sorry, Sam. But what does it have to do with me?"

"You know, this would be so much easier if you'd just read my mind. Okay, here it is... We need a sperm donor. Would you do it?"

What! Shit. What? "Donor?"

"Yes."

"You want your ugly, gay brother to be your sperm donor?"

Sam sighed. "Your scar is something you gotta deal with, Shane, and it isn't hereditary. But yes, we want you to be the donor."

"Why? Why not one of your friends from around here?" Shane motioned to their father. "Hell, why not Dad?"

Sam seemed to relax. "That would just be too creepy. You? Well, brother, whether you like it or not, we are identical twins."

Shane studied his twin. He was well aware they were similar, with darker curly hair and olive complexions. The rest of the family were fair-skinned and blond. Hope clearly flickered on Sam's face when Shane didn't turn him down immediately. Shane squeezed his eyes shut and leaned against his horse for support.

"We need to talk about something before this conversation goes any further."

"Ask whatever you'd like," Sam said.

Shane took a deep breath, his gaze going from his brother to his dad. "A lot of people around here don't trust me, but I was born gay. It wasn't a choice." Shane raised his hand to stop any comments. "Yes, it matters. Most scientists believe being gay is genetic — one way or another. So, your baby might have a more than the usual chance of being gay. Have you thought about that?"

"Yes, the doctor explained the same thing but Angie and I agree. If our baby is as great as you, then we don't care who they want to be with — like, intimately."

A lumped formed in Shane's throat. A glance at his father confirmed that he echoed Sam's sentiment. "Okay, but to be clear about this, I am not the dad. You are. I'm happy to be the indulgent uncle, though."

Sam's laugh rang through the cluster of trees. "No problem, bro. No problem."

Shane's dad pulled his horse from the grass it was nibbling at and swung into the saddle. "We better get home. Your mother will worry."

The two younger Reeses followed their dad's example and soon the trio was riding toward the ranch headquarters. Sam turned to Shane with an expression of relief. "Thanks. For everything. How are things going for you?"

Shane turned to his brother in high spirits. "Well, there is this one bull rider..."

"You have to catch me to tell me the gory details of your love life!" Sam kicked his boots against his horse's sides and shot off at a gallop.

Shane snorted and urged Dudley in pursuit, but he was more comfortable with his family than he had been in years. Now he had to work out his feelings about Dustin.

* * * *

Shane decided to stay a few more days when he realized it was time to work the cattle. Everyone helping made the task easier, but the effort had already had its effect. He slid off his straw hat and combed his sweaty hair back with his fingers as Sara forced another group of calves closer to the working chutes for vaccines and brands before they were separated from their mothers. The next few days would be loud while cows complained about missing their babies and calves were equally ticked off about losing their mothers. *If it gets bad enough, I might decide to leave tonight instead of in the morning.*

"Wake up, sleepy! There are a couple of these calves that really want to be back with their moms. They've already tested the corral once," Sara said.

Shane flipped open his gate and forced his way through the mass of four-hundred-pound calves to help Sara with the crowding gate. With both of them, it didn't take long before the animals were in the working chutes.

He and Sara kept the stream of cattle moving through to Sam and their dad. This was just one of the annual tasks they worked on together. The effort was divided across several groups of cows to keep the amount of work limited, so they finished before the heat of the day to make the effort less stressful on the people and cattle.

Surprisingly enough, it was these kinds of family efforts Shane missed most. When he and Sam had been young, they had marked a calendar on their bedroom wall with each time they'd gotten to help with the herd. Shane felt sure they had been more of a hindrance than a help those first few years. But it had been a credit to his father's patience that everyone had gotten a job they could finish.

There had only been a few disasters over the years and none of them had ended with an injury.

"Hey! You asleep back there?" Sam yelled.

Shane almost answered with colorful profanity but remembered he wasn't in a crowd of bull riders. "I'm coming! Hold your shorts."

Sara laughed as she shoved one of the calves toward him. "Seems like you're getting soft from all the town living."

The calf shot through and was caught with a bang of metal. Shane kept back any comments he might have had.

The good-natured banter continued as they finished working the last of the calves and moved them to the weaning pasture. It was close enough to keep an eye on the temperamental juveniles but far enough to give the family a break from their cries.

The last of the day's calves moved through a series of enclosures to where they would be held for the next few days. When they returned to the working pens, their dad waved them on. "Take the cows to the south eighty. They'll calm down quicker if they can't see their calves. It shouldn't take more than you two. Sara can help me clean up and get everything ready for the next batch later in the week."

Shane and Sam waited an instant to see if there would be a last-minute change before trotting over to their horses that had been relaxing under the shade of a nearby group of trees. They were avoiding Sara's glare as they rode into the pasture. They eased their way through and gathered the cows ahead of them. Once they had them moving down one of the connecting lanes, Sam drew his ride up so their horses walked side by side.

They had ridden halfway to their destination when Shane glanced at Sam and continued their ongoing conversation about Shane donating sperm. "It isn't that big of a deal. We're identical twins. It makes sense."

"It still feels kinda weird. Angie and I have been talking about it on and off for months and it's still odd."

Shane chuckled and shook his head. "Yeah, I guess it's a bit...unusual."

Sam peeled off for a minute to stop a cow who'd decided she wanted to go back to try to be with her calf. The horse leaped in front of her and brought her to a stop. She snorted and tossed her head once before turning and running to catch up with the others. Once Sam seemed satisfied he'd headed off the problem, he trotted his mount back. The awkward silence built again until Shane drew to a stop.

"What's eating at you? I don't know what else you want to hear from me."

"It's not you. I wanted to talk to you about Mom and Dad."

"What about them? They seem fine."

"They're trying to understand about you being gay. Sara and I are working on them. They don't want to lose you. Dad is pretty much there—"

"And our ultra-religious mother?"

Sam shrugged. "She's trying. She's talked to an unbelievable number of people."

"She could talk to me."

Sam twisted his lips. "It's taking her a little longer."

"And what if your child is gay?"

Sam's tone changed to something other than the typical easy-go-lucky Sam. "No one better mess with my kid. I don't want them to have the problems you went through."

Shane's expression softened. "I think we've solved all of this family's issues for now. We better get these cows situated before Dad starts hunting for us."

At a touch of their heels, their mounts jumped forward, ready to finish the job.

Chapter Seven

Dustin's pacing was wearing a path in the bland carpet of the motel room. *Where is Shane? I haven't seen him since Cody.* With another small rodeo under their belt since then, Dustin and Todd had arrived at Cheyenne, one of the biggest events on the circuit. He stopped his pacing and glanced at Todd as he walked through the room. "Hey, shit for brains, where're you going?"

Todd eyed Dustin in disbelief. "I have a towel, shampoo and I'm parading around in my underwear. Where the hell do you think I'm going?"

"Shower. Sorry, wasn't thinking." Dustin waited until the door shut then resumed pacing the sparse motel room, his emotions in turmoil. He thought about Shane constantly now. His gut twisted into knots the whirlwind of emotions the big bullfighter generated in him. This obsession for a single man was new for Dustin. He'd slept with several guys since high school when he'd started rodeoing full-time. His sex drive had always been in high gear and he'd hunted for a way to take care of it. The bull riders all knew each other, so he'd always been careful not to sleep with someone from the rodeo circuit. His family's reaction to his sexuality had made one thing clear. He couldn't trust anyone with the information.

But with Shane, everything had shifted in ways Dustin had never felt before. He'd broken his own rule in hooking up with Shane, because he was definitely part of the rodeo crowd. Dustin still wasn't sure why he'd told Shane anything. It wasn't like he'd known all that much about him, only friend-of-a-friend-type information. *Is Shane thinking about me at all?* He flopped onto the bed, struggling to figure out what was happening to him. The shower stopped and steam billowed from the bathroom when Todd opened the door.

"Damn, it feels good to get the dust washed off me. Do I have scratches down my back?" Todd turned his bare back toward Dustin. "She was a wildcat in bed. She clawed me up pretty good while I was pounding her."

Dustin glanced at his friend's back and waved him off with one hand. "Nothing bad. You've been worse off."

"Yeah, she was kinda rough." Todd flipped his towel off and started drying his hair. Dustin rubbed at his eyes and yawned. Todd was proof he wasn't attracted to everyone with a dick, because he'd never wanted to be with Todd. He couldn't say the same about Shane.

Dustin walked to the bathroom, turned on the water and stripped. After stepping under the hot spray, he soaped up, most of his thoughts still on Shane. *I have to do something. That's all there is to it. I can't keep acting like a lovesick high schooler.*

* * * *

Shane knew Dustin would be one of the riders at Cheyenne. He'd arrived from the ranch in the hope he would be able to talk with him. He'd tried the usual haunts for the bull riders with no luck. Now that the bull riding round had begun and it was Dustin's turn, Shane's heart was in his throat and the twist in his gut was tighter than a handmade lariat. He ran along the fence, staying in position so he could rush in to help if needed. The bull jumped then slammed against the ground with such force that Shane cringed. The blood-red animal launched itself again, its back arching into a crescent before uncurling to blast into the arena. It spun, turning sideways and making it more difficult for Dustin to keep his precarious seat.

Constantly in motion, Shane worked to put himself at the best possible spot to help if needed. The stakes for protecting a cowboy had never been this high. This time it was Dustin. Shane could tell this wouldn't be a high-point ride. Dustin was too close to losing control with each jump. The bull threaded its way across the arena, leaping from spot to spot, switching between spins and straight bucking.

Shane's breath caught when the bull jumped and kicked out again, getting all four feet off the ground. Shane ran closer, working out where he should be. He'd been doing this for years. He could read the bulls as well as anyone, and this ride wasn't going well. In the past, it hadn't been personal. It had been his job. That had all changed now.

The red bull was fast and fought hard. His jumps and spins cracked Dustin around like a cheap whip. Shane shifted again, eager for the buzzer to signal the ride's end. When someone he cared about was on the back of an enraged bull, eight seconds seemed to last an eternity.

Dustin's luck changed for the worse as the end of his ride sounded. The frantic yanks he was making provided Shane all the information he needed. Dustin was in trouble. Shane's job now was to make certain the screaming buzzer signaled only the end of the ride, and not Dustin's demise.

Shane launched himself toward the bull and grabbed Dustin's arm. The bull chose that instant to roll again and this time didn't regain his feet. The world spun. Shane lost his grip. Without a doubt, this ride would end in disaster. The bull landed on its back and almost on Dustin. There was a sickening thud. Shane's stomach knotted and adrenaline-fueled desperation flooded him.

The bull scrambled to its feet and shot across the arena while Shane tried to help Dustin stand. At Shane's light touch, Dustin hissed through clenched teeth. Shane walled away his feelings for Dustin to enable him to focus on his job. He switched to Dustin's uninjured side and tugged him through the open gate.

He turned to Dustin. "You need to get checked out."

Dustin lurched toward the pipe fence and grabbed it with his good hand. His jaw clenched as he tried to brush off some of the arena dirt that covered him from shoulder to knee. Shane's gut twisted with each flash of agony that flicked across Dustin's face.

"Fuck it. I'll be fine. I'll tape everything tight." Dustin winced when someone brushed against his arm.

"Hey, you gotta get it checked. Have Todd take you," Shane said.

Dustin laughed then his teeth snapped together in a grimace. "Todd ain't gonna take me. He'd tell me not to be such a pussy, throw the tape at me and tell me to cowboy up."

Shane glanced at the arena, relieved he had a few more minutes while they got the red bull out. "Okay. I have two more riders then this round ends. Stay here and I'll take you to the ER once I'm done."

"Man, really. No biggie."

Shane reached out and tapped Dustin's hand, which was met with a sharp gasp. Dustin stared at Shane with defeat in his eyes then said, "Fine, but they'll just tape it, too."

The other bullfighter called to him and Shane turned to go. "I'll be back. Hold tight for a few minutes." He waited for a nod of acknowledgment then ran back into the arena.

* * * *

Dustin lay on the examination table, pain radiating from his left side, and focused on shallow breaths so no part of his body moved. The ride to the emergency room had been one of the more miserable experiences in his life. Now his only concern was not throwing up on Shane or one of the hospital workers. Shane was in the room with him and his face was etched with concern. Cranking up his bravado, Dustin caught Shane's gaze. "This is stupid. It's just cracked ribs. There's nothing they can do about it but tape it up and let me go. I can't afford to have any time off the circuit."

"You didn't seem too good when we got here. I'm sure the painkiller has made you nice and happy, but the bull got you pretty good. You need to wait until the doc passes judgment."

"Whatever… This is still stupid."

The door swung in and the swirl of a white lab coat filled the room. The doctor smiled at Dustin. "Mr. Lewis, you were lucky. There are no broken bones on the X-rays, but we think you have a bruised liver, so we want to keep you overnight for observation to make sure there are no complications. You should be good to go in a few weeks, no more than a month."

"Month! Doc, there's no way. I got a rodeo next weekend."

The grizzled doctor lifted an eyebrow and pursed his lips. "This could become a serious injury if you aren't careful. I would recommend you follow my instructions to the letter."

Dustin pushed himself forward on the exam table but fell back when a tidal wave of agony shot through his abdomen. A large hand fell across his chest and held him in place. Shane was a warm, comforting presence.

"I'll make sure he stays in bed tonight at home, Doc. I'm an EMT and I'll keep him down until he heals."

The doctor shook his head but studied the pair. "It wouldn't be the best option, but if you're there to watch him…"

Shane glanced at Dustin and caught his air of panic. He realized that Dustin had no one to help. "Yes, I'll take care of him."

Shane walked beside Dustin as he rode in the wheelchair to the pickup Shane had parked just outside the exit. Shane enjoyed a measure of relief. Dustin's expression said the pain had decreased considerably. They'd given him enough medication that he was simply slumped against the chair with a stupefied expression.

Shane opened the door and moved him from the wheelchair onto the seat. Once Dustin was settled, Shane buckled him in and closed the door. Shane had a few concerns about taking care of Dustin. The new trailer he'd gotten at the end of his recent visit home would make for cozy sleeping arrangements but Shane knew they'd adjust. This all depended on Dustin allowing Shane's help, but Shane didn't see where Dustin had any choice. Their relationship might be in limbo, but Shane would help any way he could. He'd tried to find Todd but had had no luck. Right now, Dustin needed to keep still while they traveled to give his body time to recover. From what Shane had seen, 'still' wasn't a quality anyone would associate with Dustin. But if he wanted to make National Finals, he had to let himself heal.

Shane drove to the campground with Dustin reclined as much as his seat would let him. Dustin's pain could resurge any time. He already had his jaw clenched.

"Hang in there. I put my trailer at a state park just outside of town," Shane said.

Dustin nodded, breathing in a hiss when they hit the gravel road that made up the last half-mile of the trip.

Shane rolled to a stop in front of the tiny teardrop trailer.

Dustin grabbed the oh-shit handle above the pickup door and lifted himself up enough to get the first view of what would be his home for the next several weeks.

"What the fuck? That's not a trailer."

"Yes, it is. There's a queen-size bed and it has a tiny kitchen in the backend. I got it a few days ago when I was home. Our neighbor bought it and never used it, so my dad made a deal with him. It'll work for you until you're better."

Dustin stared at the tiny trailer. "How the hell are we gonna fit in there? I doubt I could get my gear in that thing. We'll be shoved in there tighter than a virgin."

He glanced at Shane and realized the thought of being in close quarters with him actually sounded good. *When he touches me, I want more. It's not just me being horny, either.* Shane made Dustin feel something he hadn't experienced since junior high — safe. That was when he'd realized he was what his grandfather called *'a perversion of nature doomed to eternal hellfire'* or words to that effect. What he and Shane shared might have started with the same fooling around he'd done with the other guys, but their time together had become much more. He'd thought of little other than Shane since the morning they'd enjoyed together. Dustin craved this new feeling of intimacy that he never remembered having before. But he knew there was no way Shane felt the same about him.

Dustin stared at the trailer, unwilling to meet Shane's eyes. "Todd'll take care of me. You don't need to. You barely know me."

Shane ran his fingers through his hair. "There aren't too many bull riders, and we know all you guys. Todd's not a bad guy, but I wouldn't want him taking care of me while I was busted up."

"Todd's okay. But he doesn't..." Dustin dropped his gaze before locking eyes with Shane.

When he didn't continue, Shane finished for him. "Todd doesn't know you're gay, does he? You're afraid he'll freak out when he finds out he's been sleeping in the same room with a gay guy for years."

Dustin rose from the seat and a low groan of pain escaped his lips. In spite of the agony, he remained defiant. "You don't know him. Todd was the only friend who would take me in. I'd lived in my pickup for a couple of weeks before I asked him if I could crash at his house until I got my shit together. He said I was a dumb-ass for not asking sooner, and there were never any more questions…not from him, not from his family. They never asked why I'd been thrown out. I owe them. I don't want to ruin his reputation."

Shane nodded. "Come on. We can talk about how bad our lives suck some other time. We need to get you into bed so you won't keep irritating your injuries." Shane jumped out of the truck to help Dustin. They made the short trip and stood outside the small trailer door. Shane fumbled for his keys while Dustin struggled to stay upright. Once it was unlocked, the door swung open enough for Dustin to lower himself and peer inside.

"Well, shit, it's a bed on wheels. I guess that'll work."

"Come on. You need to lie down. Let's get your shirt off first. It'll be a lot easier to do out here."

Dustin's breath caught and his heart raced at Shane's touch. The glancing contact as the first button opened, along with the wisp of cool air that curled over his hot skin, added to Dustin's already over-amped body. But with each movement, agony ricocheted through him and dampened his randy thoughts. In spite of the pain, opening the second button caused Dustin's nipples to harden and ache. By the time Shane opened the last one, Dustin had squeezed his eyes tight and his breathing was coming in gasps.

"You okay?" Shane asked.

"Yeah, it's just...been a while. That felt good...your hands."

Shane nodded but didn't comment. "Come on. Let's get you into bed. I'll make us some supper. The sun'll set soon and I don't want to cook in the dark."

"Okay. Let's get me inside this thing, then."

Dustin crawled through the small opening. Pain shot through his abdomen with each movement. With help, he got onto the bed. A few minutes passed as Dustin lay back with Shane helping to support him. Dustin moved in tiny increments until he could rest against the headboard and his misery spiraled down.

"You okay?"

"Yeah. That son of a bitch did a number on me, though. It hurts like hell to take a deep breath."

"Well, try to relax." Shane glanced at Dustin's prescription that they'd filled on the way from the hospital. "You can't take any more painkillers for an hour. I'll fix dinner."

Dustin closed his eyes, and his tension lessened. "Okay, that sounds like a plan."

Now that Shane's touch was gone, a part of Dustin resented Shane mothering him. His family had taught him the lesson of how disposable people were. Shane had no reason to care for him. Dustin struggled to figure out why. *Why do I want to curl against his chest and let him take care of me?* There was the pop of plastic ice chest opening just outside the trailer and Shane appeared at the tiny door with a dripping can of pop in his hand.

"Here. I thought you might be thirsty. I'm making us some bacon and eggs with toast for supper."

Dustin accepted the can and studied it for a minute. "Got a beer or something stronger?"

Shane gave Dustin a lopsided smile. "Sorry, bud. No booze with an injured liver. The tests came back okay, but you still don't want to push it — not if you're serious about the finals."

"Fine. I'll drink the pop. Bacon and eggs sound good." Dustin turned the cold can in his hand. He still was undecided if he wanted someone to give him the gentle protection he associated with the fading memories of his mother or if he resented the implication that he couldn't take care of himself. A few metallic bangs came from the back of the trailer and, a short time later, the smell of frying bacon curled into his nostrils. By the time Shane appeared at the door with a plate loaded with food, Dustin's stomach sounded like a lion lived inside.

"Here. It's not much, but the eggs are fresh. Mom loaded me up when I was home."

Dustin twisted around in the trailer until he sat with his hip against one wall. He cut his fork into the egg and deep yellow yolk ran out. He glanced at Shane as he crawled in beside him. "What's wrong with the eggs?"

Shane nodded toward the puddle of yolk on Dustin's plate. "Sorry. I made them the way I eat 'em. I can cook them more if you'd like."

"No, I like my eggs runny. These are a weird color, though. Why are they almost orange?" Dustin ran his fork through his plate, aware that uncertainty must be showing on his face.

"My folks have chickens running around outside. The yolks are always dark, not like those pale store-bought things. Try 'em. They taste good."

He felt like a rebellious twelve-year-old, but lifted the smallest imaginable bite to his mouth and slipped it in.

He chewed with wonder at the incredible flavor. "These are good. I was afraid it was one of those things everyone told me was great but really tastes like shit."

Dustin tore off a piece of his bread, ran it through the warm liquid yolk then popped it into his mouth. "Yeah, these're damn good. I need to add chickens to my master plan."

"Master plan?"

The heat of embarrassment flushed through Dustin. "Oh, just a fucking dumb game I play with myself. Todd says it's stupid shit."

Shane ate a forkful of eggs and bacon, studying Dustin while he chewed. "Tell me about it. It sounds cool."

Dustin shot Shane a glance. Fear filled him at sharing his dream with the guy he was falling for. After a long silence, Dustin decided it was time to take risks, at least where Shane was concerned. "It's like a wish book, for when I win the National Finals — what I'm going to do with the prize money."

Shane dragged a piece of toast across his plate, cleaning the last bit of egg yolk. "Like what?"

"Like a big ranch. A herd of cows." Dustin met Shane's eyes and shrugged. "I guess chickens now, too. Maybe a horse, though I never learned to ride."

"I thought it was against the rules for someone involved with rodeoing not to ride a horse."

Dustin nudged Shane with his elbow. "Yeah, well, they don't like gay guys in it, either, but we're making it."

A slight frown formed on Shane's face. "That's different. I've heard of guys being jumped because some idiots thought they might be gay. I haven't told too many people about me. Mostly family, and they're too embarrassed to tell anyone." Shane's expression became thoughtful. "Or at least that's the way it used to be. My siblings are cool about it, though."

Dustin set his plate on the mattress and nodded. "At least they didn't try to beat you to death or throw you out."

"No, they're getting used to it. It took them a while. My mom's still not happy, at least she wasn't the last time the subject came up. People in West Texas don't take change well."

"Some people don't take change, period." Dustin allowed himself time for a bit of introspection, then smirked at Shane. "So, what're the sleeping rules? You know I can't sleep with clothes on."

Shane laughed at Dustin and shook his head as he gathered up the dishes and backed out of the trailer door. A few minutes later Shane reappeared with two sleeping bags. He tossed them into the camper and grinned at Dustin. "Those should work so long as we're up north. When they get too hot… Well, we'll work that out when it happens."

Chapter Eight

Dustin sat in the shade beside the tiny trailer he'd been living in for the past week. His injuries had improved. He only noticed the pain sometimes after he'd pushed himself too hard. Each ache reminded him how close he'd come to being hurt worse than he had. If his injuries weren't enough proof of how dangerous rodeo was, he only had to check out the scar running down Shane's face. Dustin had played the accident over and over again in his mind. It could have come out a lot worse. *That's one thing I know for sure.* Dustin cradled the journal where his hopes and dreams lived and stared into the distance.

As he dragged himself from the dark funk, Dustin lifted his T-shirt and checked the yellow-and-black coloration covering his left side. He gently pressed a few of the more vibrant spots. *Those are still a little touchy. It's better, though. I have to ride again soon or everything will go to shit.*

"Hey, how's my favorite bull rider today?"

Dustin jumped, startled by Shane's sudden appearance. Shane stood beside him with plastic grocery bags hanging from each finger. *I have to take care of my part. He's paying for everything. He'll get tired of that shit.* "I'm fine, but you can't keep buying groceries without me giving you some cash."

"You mean I'm bringing home the bacon?"

Another pang of failure shot through Dustin. "I guess so. You're having to buy everything."

"No, I was teasing about bringing home the bacon. It's an old saying from somewhere. You know, like I'm the one who works and brings in the paycheck."

"Yeah, I get it. I don't like it. It's like I'm mooching off you."

"No. It's okay. I'm sure you'd do the same for me. I really was goofing around. Besides, I like your company while we drive all over the country."

Dustin thought for a few seconds before he shrugged. "I like riding with you, too. But from now on, I'm helping pay for my part of the expenses. Otherwise, it's not fair."

"Okay, if it's important to you." Shane motioned to the trailer. "Let me get stuff packed away and I'll start dinner."

As Shane put the food away, Dustin's tension eased. Shane moved with a powerful grace that Dustin found sexy. He relaxed into the chair, spread his legs and squeezed his package. "I'm so horny I could fuck a goat. I haven't got off in forever."

Shane watched the show, running his tongue over his lips. Dustin shot him a quick wink and rubbed his crotch. Shane glanced around, likely to make sure they were alone, then watched Dustin open his legs wider and use both hands to work his junk.

"Someone sees you and they'll call the cops."

"Ah, come on. I'm not so sore anymore. Let's play around. I'm so horny that I'd even do a cop."

Shane's face turned somber as Dustin continued groping himself. "Knock it off, Dustin. It's not cool to tease me."

"What? How am I teasing you?"

"I guess you were being nice the last time or were really horny or whatever. It's cool. I'm not pissed off or anything. But I don't want to be another notch on your bedpost."

"For such a smart guy, you sure are one dumb motherfucker sometimes. You confuse the shit outta me."

Shane crossed his arms and glared. "What do you mean?"

"You were the one who told me 'see you sometime', not the other way around. Now you're all pissy and telling me I don't want you. How do you know? 'Cause I don't know. Just give me a chance to figure out what's going on. Okay?"

Shane let out a long sigh. "It's not that easy. I have stuff—"

"Oh fuck, we all have stuff. Does your dad hate you?"

Shane winced. "No, nothing like that."

"Do I turn you on?"

"Yes, you do."

"Well, how the hell would I know either of those things? When have you told me?" Dustin asked.

"Okay, okay. I get it. But everyone else has—"

"No! Fuck, no! I'm not everybody you've ever slept with, I can guarantee you. Now, you interested in having some fun, or would you rather I deck you because you pissed me off?"

"When I talk with you it's like riding a roller coaster with nothing holding you in."

"Damn straight it is. Now, I'm going to get off. It will be a lot more fun if you'd get your ass in the trailer with me."

"Okay, all right. You're right. It's been a while since I popped one, too." Shane broke into a smile. "Besides, now that you're better, you can show me more of your moves."

Shane opened the door to their teardrop trailer. "Come on, stud. I think we can call this makeup sex after our discussion."

Dustin stood and his hard cock tented his jeans. He grabbed Shane's crotch as he walked past him to disappear through the doorway. He popped his head back outside and studied Shane. "I've never understood makeup sex. Why would you have sex with someone you're pissed off at?"

Shane put his hand on Dustin's head and pushed him back inside. "Stop talking and let me get in there, too." Shane adjusted his swollen cock before following.

By the time he crawled through the door and onto the bed, Dustin's shirt was off and his jeans were wadded around his ankles.

"Damn. Slow down a little," Shane said.

"Fuck that. I'm horny."

Shane unbuttoned his jeans, lifted his ass off the mattress and shoved his pants and underwear to his ankles. Before he could take off his boots, Dustin closed the distance between them and swallowed his cock. Shane fell back with a gasp as his cock slid into Dustin's throat like it was made for it. After weeks of wondering if the last time had just been a fluke with a horny, drunk cowboy, Shane had his answer. After Dustin had made a few trips up and down the length of his cock, he grabbed Dustin's shoulders and lifted him.

Dustin's breath came in gasps as Shane ran his hands over his eager lover. "Let me get undressed. I want to have at least a chance of getting some action, too," Shane said.

His face a whirlwind of battling emotions, Dustin nodded. He wiggled until he was at Shane's feet then tugged at his boots. Shane attempted to help before giving up and letting Dustin strip him bare. When the last sock flew through the air, he left a trail of kisses up the inside of Shane's leg. Each touch created a spark of heat that ran to Shane's crotch. By the time Dustin reached his dick, pre-cum ran down its length.

Shane tried to reach more than the shoulders of his squirming bed partner until, frustrated, he growled, "Turn around. I want some kissing before I get off."

Dustin turned until their faces were inches apart. Shane paused for an instant before easing closer. When their lips touched, waves of tingling pleasure filled his body. Soon they were devouring each other as passion built and Shane was filled with lust and wanted more. Shane pulled them apart until he could stare into Dustin's endless blue eyes.

"I want some of that tight, round butt," Shane said.

Dustin spun on the bed and moved his ass over Shane's face. Shane didn't have much experience in rimming someone. In his few times, he'd bottomed, and that had mostly been in the dark with the other guy blowing his wad as fast as possible. None of them had been concerned about Shane's pleasure. The one time he'd talked someone into letting him try anal play, the guy had passed out halfway through, which hadn't left Shane in the mood to keep going.

As always, Dustin was a ball of boundless energy and enthusiasm. Before, Dustin's attraction to him had given Shane something he'd never experienced before, a partner who found him desirable. Now he was eager to see if the intimacy survived. Truth be told, he still didn't have high expectations, in spite of Dustin's tirade. He eased his face against Dustin's dancing hips and inhaled. The scent of sweat mixed with the essence of Dustin curled through his nose. The aroma was intoxicating. He grabbed the muscular cheeks and opened them to see Dustin's pucker twitching.

Shane licked and kissed his way down the curve of Dustin's ass. By the time he was circling Dustin's entrance, the cowboy was thrashing in his hands. The heat rose and he blew across Dustin's hole.

"Oh God. That's fucking fantastic," Dustin said.

Shane squeezed Dustin's ass in his hands. "I haven't even started. Just wait."

He slapped Dustin on the butt then pressed his face between Dustin's hard cheeks. He flicked his tongue out to swirl around and over his opening until a loud moan rumbled from Dustin. The passion of their building connection drove Shane to a level of pleasure he hadn't experienced before. Focused on that goal, he licked from just under Dustin's sac to the top of his firm ass. Once Dustin was squirming, his responses confined to tiny gasps, Shane shoved his tongue inside.

"Fuck! Oh, damn it!" Dustin yelled.

Minutes of lust passed as Shane plunged his tongue into Dustin until he lay on Shane, his knees drawn up beside him, quivering and gasping. From the sounds

Dustin made, Shane expected the hot spatter of cum any second.

"Fuck me!"

Shane froze, stunned by what he'd heard. "What?"

"Fuck me, damn it. What you're doing is so good, but I need something bigger in there. I need your cock."

"I thought you didn't bottom."

"Are you going to fuck me or do I need to go find a dildo?" Dustin asked.

"Okay, okay. Whatever you want. I don't want you to regret it."

"If it's half as good as your tongue, there won't be anything to regret." Dustin popped Shane's arm. "Now, get moving!"

Shane slid from under Dustin and lunged into their storage. He burrowed through his shaving kit until he found what he was searching for. Equipped with a condom and lube, he moved to Dustin. He drizzled the slick liquid onto Dustin's butt then swirled the pooling lube around his hole.

"Oh, God. Stop teasing me, put it in," Dustin demanded.

Shane slipped his finger in to the first knuckle, pausing as Dustin's ass clenched and he let out a low moan. For several minutes, Shane worked his way deeper inside until he was sheathed in Dustin. Shane fingered Dustin until he squirmed under him, his ass clamped tight. When the vise grip on his finger lessened, Shane slipped out, lubed two fingers and repeated himself.

Dustin gasped and pushed backward. "Holy shit! Come on, Shane. Fuck me! Please!"

"Hang in there. I'm thicker than two fingers. You want to sit down tomorrow."

Dustin pressed his chest into the mattress, moaning and writhing as he shoved himself backward. Shane trapped Dustin under his hand, pinning him. "We're going at my speed. I've had it too fast and it's not as much fun as you think."

Dustin nodded and swallowed hard, his deep blue eyes begging Shane to give him what he wanted. Shane tilted his head and Dustin buried his face in the pillow before relaxing.

Once Dustin had again loosened up under Shane's careful foreplay, he eased out and added a third finger after soaking them with lube. As he pressed them against Dustin's hole, Shane worked to further loosen the tight, virginal butt. This time when he pressed forward, Dustin let out a hiss. "Damn, that burns."

"Yeah, exactly. I'd like to ram into you. I'm horny as a three-spotted goat. Trust me on this. I've had inconsiderate tops before."

Dustin knitted his brows together. "Including me?"

Shane paused for a second to recall what Dustin was talking about. "No, that was because you didn't understand. That's not the same at all."

Dustin nodded and relaxed, his eyes fluttering closed as he chewed on his bottom lip. Shane drifted, wanting this to be a life-altering experience. After a few minutes, Dustin let out the breath he was holding and sighed. "It's good now. Wow, that was fucking intense."

Shane worked his fingers in and out until Dustin moved in response again. After a few minutes, Shane let his fingers slip out.

Dustin gasped. "Damn, put 'em back in. It's so good."

Shane slapped Dustin across the ass. "Oh, wait. I have something that'll fill all the right places."

He opened the condom and unrolled it down his shaft. The tight sheath caused his cock to throb as he emptied the rest of the lube onto his dick. Shane stroked it, covering his shaft with a thick layer. Dustin dropped his chest against the mattress and stuck his ass in the air. Shane smirked and wedged his dick against Dustin's opening.

Dustin moaned loud enough to shake the tiny trailer. "Oh, God. That's so good."

His response drove Shane deeper into a sex-induced delirium. He came closer and closer to giving Dustin what he wanted as the lust boiled through his veins. He pushed forward until the head slipped in then he paused. Shane ran his hands over Dustin, leaning down to kiss the back of his neck, enjoying his smooth skin as they recovered.

He needn't have worried. Dustin pressed backward like a heifer in heat. Fulfilling the role of bull was what Shane had in mind. *Damn, he has me so fucking horny!* As Shane pressed his cock farther into Dustin, he moaned.

"Shit. You're huge!" Dustin said.

"I'm not huge. I'm not even sure I make the 'kinda big' category. But your ass is virgin tight." Shane let Dustin adjust. He rocked forward, sinking deeper each time. Shane struggled to maintain control, his breath coming in gasps. He wanted so much to make Dustin's first time an amazing memory. Time slowed and the world contracted to only him and Dustin. Shane worked his way inside a fraction of an inch at a time. When his pelvis ground against Dustin's butt, he drew back and Dustin came unglued.

"Oh fuck! Shit. Holy hell!"

Shane froze, afraid he'd hurt Dustin. "You okay? Something wrong?"

Dustin's mouth worked like a fish gasping for air before he blurted out a reply. "No. Damn. It was like peeing on an electric fence, but good."

Shane couldn't keep from giggling. He knew what had happened. *He's so damn cute. I want to hold him forever.* Shane fought to keep from lapsing into hysterical laughter. Once he got himself together, he explained. "I hit your prostate. That's the electric sensation. Good, isn't it?"

"Oh shit! It was like I was coming a little but rapid-fire. Can you hit it again? Please!"

"I'm pretty sure the nice curve you like about Junior will make it easy to hit your sweet spot."

Dustin sighed and slumped against the bed. "I like that curve. Damn, I could get addicted to this real quick."

"Well, let me try and help your addiction." Shane eased out bit by bit then sank into Dustin again. This time he aimed for Dustin's sweet spot, wanting to send him reeling. He sank inside and his cock again slid against Dustin's button.

"Oh! Fuck!" Dustin bucked and squirmed under him. Shane pinned him against the mattress then locked himself in place as he worked himself and Dustin to the edge.

"Fuck me! Quit teasing me," Dustin begged, spreading his legs wider and pushing back against Shane.

Shane ran his hands over Dustin's tight, round butt then eased out. Concern about Dustin's pleasure evaporated as Shane was overwhelmed by the hot man under him. He battled with his building desire, wanting Dustin to experience the same level of ecstasy he was. Dustin's hips shook and all question about whether or not Dustin was enjoying himself was eliminated.

"Come on. Give it to me. Harder!"

Shane lay across Dustin's bare back, grinding his chest against him. He slipped his arms around and played with Dustin's hard nipples, and when a breathy sigh leaked from Dustin, Shane curled his hips forward until he was buried inside. He worked back and forth as he screwed Dustin. His strokes came faster as the bull rider thrashed and cried out, losing control as Shane pummeled him.

Dustin struggled to get away. "Oh, fuck. No! Shit."

Shane withdrew with a snap of his hips, not sure what had happened. "Everything okay?"

"I want to see your face. I feel like a fucking bitch in heat like this."

"Turn over. If you're sure you want to see my scarred-up mug dripping sweat on you."

Dustin spun under him and wrapped his muscular legs around Shane's waist. He climbed him like a crazed monkey then Dustin sank his teeth into Shane's neck. As he bit down, the pleasure and pain created a potent mixture that surged through Shane.

"Fuck! What're you doing?"

"You're getting punished. What'd I tell you about cracks about how you look?"

Shane pushed Dustin back against the bed. "Okay, okay. No more biting."

Dustin curled close to Shane's ear and whispered, "Then fuck me."

He eased back, pausing for a heartbeat before burying his cock deep inside again. Dustin's face froze, his mouth shaped into an O, but no sound came from him. Shane worried he'd injured Dustin. He moved fractionally, clipping Dustin's hot spot, and an ear-shredding cry filled the small space.

"Oh, God, yes! Like that. Fuck me. Fuck me hard!"

Dustin raked Shane's back with his nails. The passion and pain washed over Shane. This wouldn't be a tender lovemaking. It would be a muscle-straining, butt-slapping, fuck session only two men could have. He pulled back before snapping into Dustin. Shane marked his last coherent thought with a scream. His body melded with Dustin's into a writhing mass of sweaty muscle as he raced toward the edge.

Shane erupted first then grabbed Dustin's hard nipples and twisted them. Dustin clamped his strong legs—capable of keeping him on two thousand pounds of angry bull—around Shane. Dustin rode him as Shane filled the condom.

The first molten line of Dustin's cum shot across Shane's torso as the final waves of climax washed over him. Dustin rode Shane as his body shot streams of semen. Shane's arms shook as a last tremor slid through him and he dropped onto Dustin.

Dustin threw his arms out wide. "Fuck. What did you do to me?"

* * * *

Dustin sat staring into space while Shane did the few things needed to break down the camp. Usually he helped—or at least tried to. Shane never let him do much. This time his mind was fixed on the previous night's sex. His emotions about it were far from resolved. He'd never bottomed, not for anyone. But ever since their first night in the hotel room, he'd wanted Shane to fuck him. Shane's touch, his shyness, those incredible lips… They'd changed him.

He never understood how Shane could miss how sexy he was. *He's so obsessed about that scar. I just don't get it.* Dustin lost himself in Shane's eyes every time they looked at each other. Those tiny flecks of gold flashed through them when Shane was frustrated with him. Scar and all, he found Shane so desirable. Dustin shifted in his chair and the slight ache in his butt brought his thoughts back to the night before.

Did last night change our relationship? I enjoyed bottoming for Shane. The feelings were amazing. But I like fucking, too. Have I screwed up?

Shane stood over Dustin with folded arms and a dark expression. "What're you pouting about? Something crawl up your butt?"

"Ain't nothing crawled up my butt. Leave me alone."

Shane's expression softened and he squatted in front of Dustin, his hands on Dustin's knees. "What's wrong? This isn't like you. I'd like to help."

"I'm not sure how I feel about being the bottom," Dustin blurted out.

Shane gave him a confused expression. "What?"

Dustin ran his hand over his face and glared at Shane. "You fucked me. How does that change us? You know, like we were doing a couple of things, but now I'm the bottom. How does that change…us?" There it is. *Now I've screwed up the whole thing between the two of us.*

Shane chuckled. "Who's on top and who's on bottom means nothing. They're just categories to shove someone into. None of them change what we are to each other. We decide what we do when we are being intimate, not some stupid label someone is trying to use."

"No, but that was different," Dustin stammered.

"How? How was it different?"

Dustin struggled to bring his scattered thoughts together. "I don't know. I guess because it was you, and you didn't act different afterward."

Shane's eyebrows almost merged as he stared at Dustin. "Do you feel different?"

Dustin was confused by the question. "No. I feel the same as always."

"So what do you think that means?"

Dustin shrugged, afraid he'd screwed up but not quite understanding how.

"If you enjoyed yourself then don't sweat it. Now quit being stupid, get off your ass and help me," Shane said.

Dustin moved to pack things into the back of the pickup and the trailer. He was still confused and struggling to settle on some meaning to their intimacy. He also didn't dare tell Shane he'd forgotten his Adderall. He didn't want Shane to get tired of him because he was too much trouble. Dustin got tired of taking meds all the time. He understood it helped him deal with other people, but there were times he resented it. He swore to himself he would try harder to take the meds like the doctor told him he should. That might help Shane tolerate him better.

The packing took longer than usual. Both of them were quiet, which bugged Shane, even though he knew he shouldn't let the topic bother him. His mood hadn't improved by the time they climbed into the truck to leave.

They both made a few futile attempts at conversation but none were successful. After covering several hundred miles in silence, Shane considered why he'd reacted the way he had with Dustin's questions. *Why was I short with him like that? Did his question hit too close to home?* Shane wrestled with the issue as mile after mile of hot, rolling prairie sped past their windows.

"Sorry," Shane said.

"Yeah? About what?" Honest confusion shone in Dustin's eyes.

"About being stupid earlier. There was nothing wrong with your question. I shouldn't have overreacted like that."

Dustin shrugged and turned away to stare out of the window. "Sometimes I have trouble following things. My dad always said I was about as sharp as a bowling ball."

What would I have done if my family had tossed me out like Dustin's did? At least my parents still welcomed me in their house. After my last trip home, it seemed some of them were coming to an understanding about my life.

Shane patted Dustin on the shoulder. "You aren't stupid. It's all confusing. But just because you enjoy…catching, doesn't mean you always want the same thing." Shane reached out and gripped Dustin's shoulder. "Calm down. We're lucky to find each other and have a good time. But I want to talk with you and I don't want to do it while we're flying down the interstate."

At the next exit, Shane turned off the highway and into a deserted parking lot. He killed the pickup engine and turned to Dustin. He reached over with a smile, grabbed Dustin's leg and squeezed it. "Don't get upset. It's not anything bad. At least, I don't think it is."

Dustin swallowed hard and met Shane's eyes. "Okay, what do you need to tell me?"

"I like you, Dustin."

Dustin sat frozen then slowly nodded. "I like you, too. You're a cool guy."

Shane shook his head. "No, I mean I really like you. I mean I want to be more than convenient fuck buddies."

Dustin stared at Shane with his mouth hanging open, his brows almost to his hairline. "You mean, like dating? Like going steady?" He twisted in the seat, his eyes flicking to the floorboard. "I haven't ever done that, with anyone."

Shane grinned then reached over and grasped Dustin by the back of his neck. "I guess that's as good a description as any. Maybe we'll just say we're dating. Going steady sounds a bit like we sit next to each other on the bus coming home from junior high."

Dustin relaxed under Shane's hand. "I guess that is something kids would say." He considered Shane. "So—like, you're my boyfriend?"

Shane eased them together. As their lips met, a spark of electricity raced through him. The depth of emotions building inside Shane brought up feelings he'd never experienced before. Shane eased away and noticed Dustin's cock had formed a noticeable lump in his jeans.

Reaching down, Shane squeezed it, and his heart quickened at Dustin's gasp. "Yes, like your boyfriend. That's easier to tell people than smoking-hot lover."

Dustin crumpled against the seat when Shane released him. He stared at Shane as the words sank in. "Yup, probably is better than smoking-hot lover."

"It's good. We have time and we have to talk to each other when any problems come up." They kissed again and Dustin's eyelids were fluttering when they separated.

"Yeah, we'll need to talk with each other."

Chapter Nine

Dustin spent the first few hours after their talk sitting quietly and Shane left him to his thoughts. By the time they'd crossed the Oklahoma border, Dustin had fallen asleep against the pickup door. He'd mumbled and snored a bit while Shane covered the remaining miles to their first destination.

A few hours later, Dustin stretched and his eyes fluttered open. "Where are we?"

"Southwestern Oklahoma, and you better hope the a/c doesn't conk out, because it's a hundred and five outside."

"Damn, that's worse than at home this time of year." Dustin stretched again, tweaked Shane's nose and dropped back against the door. "So where are we headed? Because this doesn't seem like the way to the next rodeo."

Shane shook his head. "I met a couple of guys early last summer and their place is close. They're selling some of their Santa Gertrudis bulls as bucking stock. That's my dream someday — to own a ranch and sell high-dollar bulls to stock contractors. You said raising cattle was in your master plan. I thought we could stop by and check out their operation. I called the last time we stopped and Mitch said it'd be fine if we came by."

"How good are the bulls?"

"Well, I think the red bull that stepped on you was one of theirs." Shane tried not to relive those horrible minutes, but he could sense the arena again as it came back to him — Dustin's yell, the snort and pivot of the bull. *Stop it! Reliving it won't change a damn thing. Dustin's fine.* "One contractor introduced me to Mitch. Someone told him I wanted to set up something similar. He's a nice guy and knows a lot about business, rodeo stock and raising cattle. I think his husband teaches at the local college or something. I've never met him."

Dustin twisted in his seat and stared at Shane. "Husband? They're *married*?"

"Apparently. I didn't pump him for information about their relationship. Why? Would that matter?"

"No, I've just never met a real-life gay couple."

"What do you think we are?"

Comprehension spread across Dustin's face. "Oh. Yeah. I guess that was kinda dumb."

Shane reached up and popped Dustin's ball cap so it tilted down over his forehead. "Not dumb. If I can't say I'm ugly then you can't say you're dumb."

Dustin smirked. "Dumb and Ugly. Sounds like a bad movie."

Shane's expression went deadpan then he laughed. "Yeah, you've got a point. Maybe we'll figure out another name for the two of us."

Dustin bounced a little in his seat. "Yup. Wonder what these guys are gonna be like."

Shane shook his head at the speed Dustin shifted from one topic to the next. It left him baffled at times.

After having spent most of the day traveling through the summer heat, Shane was excited to pull in to the ranch headquarters as the broiling Oklahoma sun touched the western horizon. Shane rolled to a stop in the parking area. As he opened the cab, he was met by a red-and-white border collie whose tail swept the ground behind him.

"Max! Leave him alone!"

Shane glanced up to see Mitch trotting toward them.

Mitch gave them a broad smile and shook hands. "Hey, Shane. Glad you stopped by. Don't mind Max. Our foster son's off with his husband on their anniversary, so we're watching the grand-dog." Dustin came around the front of the pickup. Mitch extended his hand again and grabbed Dustin in what Shane guessed was an equally firm handshake. "Hey, nice to meet you. I'm Mitch. I kinda run the ranch."

Dustin seemed to consider Mitch for a moment before he came alive. "Yeah. Hey. I'm Dustin."

"Yes, Dustin Lewis. I recognize you from TV. You're doing kick-ass in the earnings."

"I was until a bull stepped on me a few weeks ago. I've been gimping along ever since."

Mitch shook his head. "Damn bull riders. Y'all are all crazy."

A mischievous expression covered Dustin's face. "Being crazy helps. Or just so antsy that you gotta be doing shit all the time, like me."

Shane put his arm over Dustin's shoulder and turned to Mitch. "Do you still have time to show us your operation? I know the phone call was short notice."

Mitch waved his hand. "No problem. Let me tell Darrin where we're going and we'll head out."

A few minutes later they piled into Mitch's pickup and were driving across the open prairie. Dustin rode in the bed and Shane sat up front with Mitch, one arm draped over the side. As they chatted, Shane studied the deep red of the gullies and washes, punctuated by a sea of gray-green buffalo grass that ran as far as the eye could see. The islets of blackjack, post oak and cedar formed spots of relief. A handful of minutes later, they drew up beside a group of mahogany-colored cattle.

Mitch stuck his hand out of the window and rubbed a cow on the nose. She answered back by sticking out a long tongue and trying to curl it around his hand. "Hey! I don't have anything for you. Keep that tongue in your mouth."

Shane enjoyed watching the persistent animal. Mitch teased her for a few seconds and turned back to them. "They don't act like typical rodeo stock, do they?"

Shane cocked an eyebrow. "No, they don't. I expected them to be a lot crazier than this bunch."

"Well, Princess here is tame. You have to watch some of the others when you get too close to their calves or they'll nail your ass. And the bull we use for bucking stock isn't with these. I stay in the pickup or on horseback when he's around. He's protective of his herd. I'm not sure it's worth all the effort to keep him."

"Can we see him?" Dustin asked through the back window.

Mitch twisted in the seat and glanced back at Dustin. "Sure, if you'd like. That bunch is closer to the house, so we can keep an eye on them."

Mitch drove the pickup in a wide circle around the grazing animals before heading back to the headquarters. A few gates and a short drive later, Shane and Dustin stood on a high metal fence, studying a small group of massive animals.

"Which one will eat you alive?" asked Dustin.

"That darker one with the crazy horns. The other three are big babies that'll eat cattle cubes out of your hand."

"What did you have to change to start with the bucking stock?" asked Shane.

Mitch pushed his hat back and scratched his head. "Not much, really. We're trying to select ones that perform in the arena but aren't crazy." He paused again then shrugged. "We beefed up the working facilities, but that's about it. Otherwise, we treat them like the rest of the herd."

The trio continued talking about the ranch and cattle until a voice came from the house.

"Hey, supper's ready. Y'all come eat."

Shane turned to head back to the pickup. "Oh, hey. We didn't mean to intrude like this. It's about dark. We'll head out."

"You have to stay now." Mitch motioned toward the figure waiting for them. "Darrin will be pissy for weeks if you don't stay after he fixed supper. He'll swear it was something I did to run you off."

Shane glanced at Dustin. "I wouldn't mind not eating hunched up in the trailer or the pickup. What do you think?"

"All right. I don't want Darrin pissed. It would probably make the breeding stock higher if we were to come back to buy cattle from you."

Mitch waved them ahead of him. "You've got that right."

* * * *

A few hours after Darrin's wonderful dinner and a relaxing evening of good conversation, Dustin sat on the edge of the huge bed in Mitch and Darrin's guest room, uncertain how they'd ended up staying. The older couple had insisted he and Shane spend the night and enjoy an evening out of their tiny trailer. Shane and Mitch had hit it off and Dustin had enjoyed a comfortable conversation with Darrin. At first he'd been intimidated by the college professor. Dustin hadn't done well in school, but he'd soon relaxed when Darrin had talked to him like they were old friends.

"It was nice of them to invite us to spend the night," Shane said as he emerged from the bathroom.

"Yeah, they seem like guys who'd be fun to be around. I wasn't too sure at first, but I think they're okay."

Shane sat beside Dustin and bumped him with his shoulder. "So…are you okay?"

Dustin scrunched his eyebrows together, a little confused as he studied Shane. "Yeah, I'm fine. Why?"

"Well, this morning you were freaking about last night."

"Oh." He turned away. "I guess it's like you said. It's just that we're wired a bit differently. Whatever we decide works for us is right." He shot Shane a wicked smile. "Besides, it was *so* amazing."

Shane ran his hand over Dustin's back, creating electric chills with his touch. "I'm not sure about the wiring thing, but it feels good if I'm catching or pitching."

Dustin glanced around the room then wiggled his brows at Shane. "This bed's huge, bigger than the whole trailer."

"Dustin! We can't screw around here. They'll hear us."

He leaned over and ran his tongue up the side of Shane's neck. Dustin toyed with Shane's earlobe between his teeth. After a few seconds, Dustin released Shane and nibbled down his neck. He was rewarded with a soft moan.

"I promise to be quiet. Not a peep out of me."

"Damn it, Dustin. We shouldn't."

Dustin grabbed the tail of Shane's T-shirt and tugged it over his head. His short, curly hair rippled from the collar as the shirt landed on the floor. Dustin pushed him onto the bed and swung his leg over to straddle him. He ran his hand over Shane's rugged torso and toyed with the patch of hair between his nipples. Dustin scooted lower, lay on top of Shane and put his head on his chest to listen to the comforting thump of his heart. "You know that no one ever let me do this?"

Shane ran his hand down the center of Dustin's back. "Let you do what?"

"Cuddle. They wanted to fuck and run. I like cuddling with you."

A deep rumbling laugh erupted from Shane. "I'm happy to cuddle with you anytime. We don't even have to have sex if you don't want."

Dustin snapped his head up and considered Shane. "But I like sex."

Shane stroked Dustin's cheek. "Yeah, I picked up on that. I don't have a problem with getting down and dirty, either."

"Can we?"

"Dustin..."

"Come on. They're sound asleep by now. I promise to be quiet."

Shane chewed on the corner of his mouth. "I smell."

"They have a huge shower. We could both fit."

"Well...you *are* fun to shower with."

Dustin bounced on Shane's stomach. "Come on. It'll be fun."

One of Shane slid one eyebrow upward. "You'd have to be quiet. I don't want to offend these guys."

Dustin sat on top and ground his ass against Shane's crotch. He traced a cross over the left side of his chest. "Cross my heart. I'll be quiet as a mouse, but I'm really horny." Dustin reached between Shane's legs, grabbed his dick and squeezed. "Seems like you are, too."

"It's hard to keep from being horny when your boyfriend is bouncing up and down on your dick."

Dustin's heart pounded a little harder and a catch formed in his throat. "I like that."

"What? The bouncing on me?"

"Yeah, that, too. But I like it when you call me your boyfriend. No one has before."

Shane rolled and pinned Dustin under him. With a gentle touch, Shane opened the buttons on Dustin's shirt and exposed his chest. He leaned in and traced his tongue around Dustin's nipples, first one then the other. He ground their crotches together while he pressed his lips against Dustin's.

Shane panted as he ran his hand down Dustin's throat. "Okay, but if they hear us, you have to deal with them." He leaned down again and flicked his tongue over Dustin's Adam's apple. "Besides, you stink, too. Let's go enjoy the shower before we're back to washing up in public restrooms at state park campgrounds."

Dustin grabbed Shane's face and drew him in for a hard kiss. He released Shane, feeling ornery. "I'd let you fuck me in the public shower."

Shane smacked Dustin on the side of his bare chest. "You would, but I'm not willing to go to jail for sex. Come on. Let's get in that shower."

Shane peeled off his shirt and jeans, tossing each piece into a growing pile. Dustin watched, enjoying the sight of Shane's sexy body. When Shane's foot popped out of his jeans, Dustin undressed, too. He plopped to the floor and tugged at his boot. Shane tugged off the last sock and moved to help Dustin. He grabbed the heel of the boot and tugged. Soon Shane dropped the boots to the floor while Dustin threw off the rest of his clothes like something infested by a nest of red ants. Dustin grabbed Shane in a hot kiss then hauled him into the bathroom.

Dustin ran his hands over Shane's bare skin, teasing him while Shane tried to adjust the water temperature. "Stop, you horn dog, or I'll finish before we even get in the shower."

Dustin grabbed Shane's ass and squeezed. The texture under his palms sent tingles through him. He kissed Shane between his shoulder blades and whispered into his ear, "You recharge quick. We could try for a twofer."

Dustin spun as Shane yanked him into the cascade of water.

"What the fuck!"

Shane slapped his hand over Dustin's mouth and stepped behind him. "Shh! Be quiet."

"Well, don't yank me under the damn cold water. Kinda took me by surprise."

"Okay, no more surprises. But you gotta be quiet."

"Okay. Can I check you out some more?" Dustin asked.

"What do you think we're doing now?" Shane replied.

Dustin said, "No, like...really study you. I thought maybe—"

"I still don't get why you like checking me out so much. I'm all scarred up." Shane held up his hands to fend Dustin off. "I know you said the scars don't matter. I just don't understand."

Dustin froze in place, his desire for Shane almost overwhelmed by his sudden understanding. *He still doesn't get it.*

"They do matter. I think they make you even sexier." Dustin ran his finger along the side of Shane's face, not quite touching the ragged scar. The touch fanned the fire growing in Dustin.

Shane caught his hand. "That's stupid. How can scars be sexy?"

"Not stupid. It's no different than a tattoo. Those are only scars. Or the guys who brand themselves. How're those different? Besides, I think they say something about you, like how hard you fight to get what you want. You know, like when life kicks you in the nuts, you get right back up and go at it again. Most people don't do that."

Shane shrugged. "They seem ugly to me."

"Not me, so deal with it." Dustin smacked the side of Shane's bare hip.

Confusion filled Shane's face before he shrugged. "I guess I don't care. If you're getting off on it, it shouldn't matter to me."

"Exactly. Now sit down and let me check you out."

Dustin soaped up the washcloth, knelt in front of Shane and lifted one foot. He traced his finger between Shane's long toes, scrutinizing each joint and curve. Dustin used the soapy cloth and ran it over each crevice on Shane's feet until he sighed, leaned back against the wall and closed his eyes.

Dustin moved to the other foot and repeated his routine. He loved little discoveries, like the tiny patch of hair on the top of each big toe. Running the cloth up Shane's calves, Dustin mixed the white suds with the thick hair of Shane's lower legs. Shane spread his legs wider as Dustin soaped his thighs. Each time Dustin moved close to Shane's balls, a stream of pre-cum ran from his hard cock. After he scrubbed Shane's legs clean, Dustin leaned in and swirled his tongue around the crown of Shane's dick.

A deep rumbling sound came from Shane. "That's good."

Dustin eased off and squeezed the base of Shane's cock. Veins bulged along the curve as Dustin's grip tightened. Shane's groans got louder and Dustin silenced him with a kiss. "Shhh, don't wake the old guys."

Shane trembled when Dustin soaped his chest. The heat of their touch added to Dustin's building lust. He lost himself in his newfound freedom to explore, and the loving attention appeared to have its effect on Shane. He leaned close, kissed Shane's scar and ran the cloth over his face.

Shane sputtered and blew soap out of his mouth. "Hey. I haven't had my mouth washed out with soap since I was ten and my dad heard me say 'shit'."

Dustin washed the soap from his face then pressed himself against Shane. Dustin's breath came in quick gasps as his cock jerked with each touch. He pressed his lips against Shane in an urgent kiss. Dustin trapped Shane against the wall and rammed his tongue against Shane's lips. They parted and Dustin plunged his tongue in. He enjoyed the flavor he associated with Shane. The buildup of passion had Dustin rubbing his leaking cock across Shane's stomach as the water spilled over both of them. Dustin's orgasm drew close, but tonight he didn't want it to end that fast.

He stepped away, let the pounding water wash over him and curled his lips into a snarl. "Arms up. I'll scrub those pits."

Shane lifted his arms with seductive slowness, intertwining his fingers behind his head and exposing his dark armpits. The cascading water flowed along his arms and through the curls under them. Dustin licked his lips at the sight and moved closer. He lifted the dripping cloth and rubbed over the wet hair. Once he'd finished under both sides, Dustin dropped the cloth to the floor and pressed his face against Shane's neck. He explored it with his tongue and relished the faint hint of masculinity. The knot of passion in his gut expanded until he was overflowing.

Dustin rinsed Shane and kissed him again. "Let's move this to the bedroom."

"Oh no, we're doing something else first, cowboy," Shane said.

Shane lifted Dustin so he crouched facing the glass, ass cheeks spread, cock hard and balls dangling. *Shit.*

This is making me even harder. "What're you going to do?"

Shane retrieved the hand shower, changed the setting to a solid stream, then aimed at the cleft in Dustin's butt. "We're going to get you all sparkly clean, then I'll rim your ass and fuck you until you scream like a mare getting bred."

The spray of water traveled across Dustin's hip. When it pounded on his tight pucker, he dropped his head and let out a loud moan. The tingle traveled through his body and he slipped into an abyss of pleasure. Dustin almost came when Shane grabbed his balls and washed them. The rough texture of the washcloth added to the already overwhelming tightening. Dustin spread his legs wider, wanting more. His shoulders slumped and he arched his back. He struggled to find the combination that would give him sweet release. Shane ran his thick finger across his hole. Dustin jumped, his groin clenching as his dick locked and a drop of pre-cum ran from the tip. His muscles released, then seized, sending him to the edge. Cold water flooded over him and the wonderful buzz vanished.

"Shit! That's like ice."

Shane turned off the water with a smirk. "You were about to come, so I did the same as we do when a dog at home is in heat — dumped cold water on you."

"Asshole." Dustin eased himself down, his strained muscles complaining as he moved from his awkward crouch. As he turned to Shane. "It didn't exactly make me lose my boner."

"I wasn't trying for that. I just didn't want you to come in the shower."

Dustin did an internal check and nodded. "Okay, your stunt worked, and I was about to come. But next time you hose me down...watch your back."

Shane grabbed Dustin's stiff member and drew him to the bedroom. "I'll make myself a note. Now, let's dry off, because if it's all right with you, I'm about to screw your brains out."

"Oh, fuck. Yes. Now!"

A small sigh escaped Dustin as Shane shifted inside. He grabbed a towel that Shane had snagged from the bathroom and dried him. The ripple of muscle under his caress soon had Dustin's desire back to a fever pitch. Once he'd wiped off the last water droplets from Shane's skin, he tossed the towel toward the bathroom door.

Shane paused before he dried Dustin. The push and tug of the towel under Shane's strong hands had Dustin's body responding as it always did. He was filled with exquisite pleasure and heat built in his groin. Dustin closed his eyes so he could appreciate every spark of passion going through him. He sucked his breath through his teeth as Shane ran his hands up his inner thighs. After Shane used the towel to dry the last of the water from his back, Shane pushed Dustin backward to land on the bed. He bounced, his cock waving as his nipples contracted to small, hard points. He felt like a yearling colt in the presence of the herd stallion when Shane crawled across the bed.

Without a word, Shane lifted Dustin's legs and opened his butt cheeks. There was a pause. Dustin's breath caught at the hope Shane would give him what he wanted — what he needed. His tension built as Shane leaned closer until his hot breath drifted across Dustin's butt. Dustin froze as their eyes met.

"You still want this? We can stop if you aren't ready," said Shane.

Dustin wiggled down the bed, ready to beg if that was what it took to get screwed. "No. Yes. Oh fuck, whatever. Just shove something in my ass."

A soft groan drifted from him as a jolt of electricity shot through his body when the tip of Shane's tongue pierced his opening. In a few short minutes, he was giving a chorus of whimpers and moans until Shane shoved a pillow over his face. "Shh! Yell into this if you have to, but don't wake them up."

Dustin grabbed the pillow and bit down on the corner as Shane worked his ass. Shane drove his flicking tongue deeper and deeper, creating lightning that crawled along Dustin's nerves until his eyes rolled back and a familiar churning began. His breakneck race toward climax halted when Shane stopped.

"Oh, God. Don't quit. I was *so* close." Dustin reached down to his crotch and jerked himself as he ached for release. Shane wrapped his hands around his wrists and pinned them against the bed.

"Oh no. You don't get to do that. You keep your mitts away from the goods." Shane lifted each hand and kissed Dustin's palm. "Now, be still while I get the condom on."

"Just do it. Forget the fucking condom."

Dustin squirmed into the bed, his lust growing, trapped under Shane's greater bulk. Their eyes locked. There was no way Dustin could miss the expression of concern on Shane's face.

Confusion flooded Dustin. "What's wrong?"

"I wish we didn't need to use condoms," Shane said.

Dustin struggled against him. Shane's lecture was pissing him off and ruining his buzz. "Whatever, come on and do it."

"Dustin, are we a couple?"

Dustin's fury dissolved into turmoil at the apparent change in topic. "Sure. Yeah, we're a couple. You told these dudes I was your boyfriend."

"Dustin, I don't like to share. I don't want to use condoms."

Dustin wrinkled his forehead, the scent of Shane's hot body wafting over them, making it difficult to focus on the conversation. "What do you mean?"

"I don't want to be with anyone but you. If we're a couple, I don't want you sleeping with some other guy."

After finally understanding what Shane was saying, Dustin moved until their faces were only inches apart. "You're the first dude who's acted like being with me was more than just sex. I notice stuff with you I've never felt with anyone else. With the other guys, it was fuck and run, but I like cuddling with you and waking up in your arms. I don't want to share, either."

"As soon as we can, we'll get tested, then no more condoms."

"No more condoms... Sounds awesome!"

Shane flicked his tongue out and licked Dustin's nose. "Cool. But tonight, I gotta get the rubber on or no sex. We've both been with other people and we don't want to risk STDs."

"Okay, okay. Get the raincoat on and let's get going."

Shane moved to get the condom and Dustin rolled to his side to savor the show. Shane unrolled the rubber down his length then slathered his cock with lube. He caught Dustin staring and gave him a lecherous wink.

"I want to see you this time. You're so hot when you're all sexed up," Shane said as he moved between Dustin's legs.

"Yeah, you make me all hot and fuck hungry."

Shane shook his head. "Fuck hungry?"

Dustin coiled toward Shane and popped him on the shoulder. "Seriously! Shut the hell up and *fuck* me."

Shane squirted lube down the crack of his ass and teased the slick gel over him until Dustin's moans reached a new high. As Dustin squirmed, Shane pressed a slick finger into Dustin's hole and eased inside his ass.

"Ah fuck, that's so sweet."

Shane slid his finger out and repeated his work with two fingers. He grinned at Dustin. "How's that? You think you're ready?"

"Fuck. If you don't do it, I'm going to jump you," Dustin said through gritted teeth.

Shane cocked an eyebrow, thrust his fingers inside and worked Dustin until he pulled them out a short time later. Shane grabbed Dustin's thighs. With a twist of his body, Shane pressed his cockhead against Dustin's hole then Shane snapped his hips forward.

Dustin gave a silent scream as a luscious mix of pleasure and pain raged through his body. He arched up, showing he wanted more as a storm of ecstasy roared down him with more power than a prairie tornado. The euphoria filled him as he built toward a wall-shaking scream. Dustin grabbed the pillow and shoved his face into it.

Shane waited a few seconds and pressed forward, impaling Dustin on his curved length. He thrashed like a calf at the end of a rope. After a final push, Shane's wiry pubic hair ground against his ass. He whimpered and groaned into the pillow, trying to contain the sounds of his pleasure. Shane caressed his squirming body until he surfaced from his lust-induced fog.

"Ready for sex, cowboy?"

Dustin's breath seeped into the pillow as he shuddered, his entire body trembling. Delicious friction flooded Dustin as Shane pulled back then slid his cock through Dustin's opening. Shane drove back inside and Dustin lost control, groaning into the pillow as Shane plowed against his sweet spot.

Dustin lifted his head, gasping and moaning. "Oh fuck! That's it."

Shane grabbed Dustin's ankles and rammed inside. Their teasing foreplay had him close to the edge. When Shane hammered into his prostate again, Dustin erupted and covered them in jets of cum. With a final tightening of his muscles, Dustin emptied his load. He sagged against the bed with a groan of contentment.

Shane ran his tongue over his lips and dug what felt like furrows into Dustin's thighs with his fingers as he rotated inside. They lay together for several minutes with Shane making short thrusts. Dustin reveled in the scents and feel of the semen covering him, and his dick responded. A few more bumps from Shane and Dustin was again rock hard.

Dustin leered. "Quit being a wimp. Fuck me."

Shane's head snapped up and his eyebrows lifted. "You want it, hotshot?"

"Give me whatever you got. I can take your best."

A lecherous grin flowed across Shane's face. "We'll see." He adjusted his grip on Dustin's thighs and slammed forward.

"Ah, hell!" Dustin yelled.

Shane slipped back and slammed in again while Dustin wrapped the pillow around his face. His guttural screams were barely muffled, but Dustin no longer cared. Flashes of electricity shot through his body with each slam of Shane's hips. The growing ecstasy threw Dustin into a dream state.

Dustin grabbed Shane's nipples and twisted them. He grinned when Shane trembled, knowing he neared the limits of his restraint. Dustin clawed down Shane's chest, loving the pounding his bullfighter was delivering. Shane's grip on Dustin's thighs tightened as he ground his crotch against Dustin's butt. His body twitched with each wave of orgasm. Shane eased out of Dustin and collapsed on the bed beside him. "Oh my God."

Dustin ran his hand over his chest, coating it with cum that he then smeared over his hard cock. He turned to Shane. "Damn, you make me so horny."

Dustin flogged his dick and the room filled with the sounds. Shane yanked Dustin's hands off and wrapped his own around it. "Mine."

Shane stroked Dustin, running his hands through the cum on Dustin's torso to re-coat it. With a tight grip on Dustin's cock, Shane eased his hand up and down its hard length, teasing Dustin toward another orgasm.

"Come on. Jerk it. I'm so fucking close!"

Shane slapped Dustin's hands away. "Nope, it's my turn."

"Please, faster. Just a little."

Shane slowed his movement to a crawl. "Did you say slow down?"

"Ah, damn it. You asshole!" Dustin thrust his hips upward, trying to find relief.

The soft sound of Shane's laughter surrounded Dustin. *Fuck! I'm so getting even.* When Shane twisted his fist around Dustin's cockhead, it was the breaking point. Dustin's first shot arched above his torso and landed back on his chest with a wet splat. His body twitched and short, thick strands of cum ran from his cock to pool on his abdomen. The delicious final waves of orgasm flowed through Dustin, leaving him exhausted and content.

He lifted himself when Shane slid between his legs and sucked his softening cock into his mouth. Dustin relished the warm sensation as Shane licked him clean. But soon the stimulation reached a point where the slightest touch made him feel as if he were about to fly apart and he grabbed Shane's head.

"No, stop! It's sensitive."

Shane came off Dustin's flaccid member. "You're good, then?"

Dustin tugged Shane beside him and their mouths met. Dustin licked his lips, catching the faint taste of his own cum layered with the sense of Shane. "Yes. Very, very good."

Shane's gaze traveled down their bodies to the full condom hanging from his softening dick. "I think we need another shower."

Dustin leaned in and licked a speck of cum from Shane's chest. "Yeah, I think you're right."

Chapter Ten

Dustin rocked back and forth on the tailgate of Shane's pickup. Even the short drive from Mitch and Darrin's to the northern Oklahoma location of the 101 Rodeo had given him too much time to think. Now that the bull riding was about to begin, his head wasn't in the right place. If things had been normal, he would be at the arena trading insults with the other bull riders. Dustin was always keeping an eye out for anything that might give him an edge. Not today. He'd dressed an hour ago. He'd checked and double-checked each piece of tack and his bull rope was rosined and ready.

The flood of adrenaline that normally had him ready to climb the walls was missing. Dread formed an icy block to replace the competitive fire that typically burned in his belly. *Have I lost my nerve? It isn't like I haven't seen other guys get fucked up and never have the guts to climb on again.* His injury had healed. The doctor's release was stored inside the trailer. Regardless of what it said on that sheet of paper, cold apprehension looped through Dustin until he found himself immobilized with anxiety.

Todd walked up beside him and shoved on his boots. "Hey, loser. Why aren't you at the arena messing with people's heads?"

"Hey, Todd. Nice ride last weekend."

"Yeah, I was on fire. You're gonna have to kick it in gear to catch up with me."

Dustin gave a lopsided grin. "Yeah, whatever. I can whip your scrawny ass without even trying."

Todd checked a buckle on his chaps. "That why you're sitting out here trying to find the guts to climb back on a bull?"

"Fuck you!"

"Fuck you, Lewis. Tell me I'm wrong."

Dustin glared at his friend but said nothing.

"Exactly, now suck it up and let's go."

Dustin's bravado evaporated. "What if something goes wrong?"

Todd let out a bark of laughter. "It's rodeo. Something always goes wrong."

"Yeah, I get it. But it's different now."

Todd's gaze bored into him and made him squirm. When he met his friend's eyes, he seemed more serious than any time Dustin could remember. But Todd's next question shook Dustin to his core.

"So, what's up with you and the bullfighter?" Todd asked.

Dustin struggled to keep from panicking. *Shit. What's he heard?* He said, "Just friends, you know. Drinking buddies. And we were —"

Todd seated himself beside Dustin and patted his knee. "I'm not as stupid as I act. I know there's something between you two. I'd understand better, but you've been kinda avoiding me."

Dustin's stomach coiled into a solid knot as he glanced at his best friend. *How am I supposed to tell him something I've been hiding since I was ten?* Dustin took a deep breath.

"Todd, I'm gay."

"Yeah, I know," his friend replied.

"What do you mean you know? How did you know?"

Todd laughed, a happy, comical sound. "Dude, you've been checking out guys since we hit puberty. How could I *not* know?"

"Sorry, dude."

"Don't sweat it. If my wet-dream girl had been standing in front of me, I'd check her out, too."

Dustin bumped against his friend. "Yeah, whatever. You ain't all that."

Todd shoved back and punched at Dustin's arm. "Whatever. Now, you and Shane are doing the nasty? I hear he gives mean head to anyone who'll drop 'em."

"Hey!" Dustin jumped off the tailgate and drew back to punch his friend. "Watch your goddamn mouth."

Todd held out his hands. "Okay, okay! I wanted to see how serious you are about him. I haven't heard anything, but you answered my question."

Dustin paused and the anger bled out of him. "Yeah, I guess. We're kind of…together."

"Like dating?"

"Yeah, something like that."

"Well, do you tap it anywhere else?"

"No! That's not cool."

"Okay. Calm down, lover boy." Todd studied Dustin before he started again. "You're crazy, the way you ride bulls. You do stupid shit. Take insane risks."

"I'm just having a little fun."

Todd shook his head. "Dude, it's like...you want the bull to take you out."

Dustin started to argue but realized that would only get him more grief. "I dunno. It's not like I've had much to live for. I mooch off you and your family or live in motels. My pop and granddad made it clear I was worthless."

"Fuck them. They're insane. And my folks love you. I mean it. They love you like a son."

"But they don't know I'm..." Dustin threw his hands out, unwilling to say the word again, as if it might change Todd's response. "When they find out, they'll never want me to come into their house again."

"You idiot. They're the ones who asked me. They worry about you all the time—afraid you're barebacking it and will get some nasty shit."

"Your folks worry about me?" A part of Dustin warmed at the idea that Todd's family had known he was gay and still cared about him.

"Hell, yes! God, you're so stupid sometimes."

Dustin flipped off his friend. "Fuck you!"

"Yeah, you'd like to but I don't swing that way. I like pussy too much." Todd winked, then his expression changed to one of sympathy. "You like this guy, don't you?"

"Yeah. I really do. He's...cool."

"What's scaring the shit outta you, then?"

Dustin started to speak several times then collapsed with a sigh. "What happens if I get hurt bad? Shane and I are just getting to know each other."

Todd watched him with his lips pursed. "You love him?"

Dustin tensed, ready to deny it out of habit. The wave of longing for Shane crested over him and with a whoosh of breath, the tension seeped out. "Yeah, I love him. But he doesn't get it. He thinks that damn scar makes him some kind of butt-ugly perv."

"What scar?"

Dustin lifted his head to see Todd with an ornery expression on his face then shook his head. "Asshole."

"Here's the deal like I see it. You haven't cared if you lived or died before — which, by the way, pisses off your friends."

Fear and uncertainty washed through Dustin. "Yeah?"

"Yeah. Now you have a reason to get your shit together and not give me a goddamn ulcer before I get to twenty-five from worrying about your ass. You have Shane. Are you going to wimp out when you're this close to finals? Or are you going to grow a pair and ride like a mad man, but not be one?"

Dustin lunged at Todd and wrapped him in a massive hug. "Thanks."

Todd returned the hug with equal ferocity. "You asshole. I'm always here to save your butt."

Dustin leaned back, a tear rolling down his cheek. "Thanks for the understanding shit, too. I was afraid if I told you I'd lose my best friend."

Todd punched Dustin in the arm. "Dumb-ass. Come on and we'll see if you can keep up with me today."

Dustin went to an arena where he had been many times, but this time he watched the rodeo clowns in action. With Shane being his focus, Dustin stood on the bottom pipe of the fence and smiled as Shane cut up with the barrelman for the crowd, his huge overalls and giant red handkerchief flapping in the Oklahoma wind. Dustin enjoyed the routine even more knowing Shane rarely did the comedy drill. When the handsome bullfighter stuck his butt in the air and wiggled it, Dustin licked his lips as he thought about what they'd do later.

"You're drooling."

Dustin sensed Todd standing beside him. "Yeah, like what would you know about it?"

"Hey, there's a hot little barrel racer that just doesn't get what a stud I am. I understand what it's like to get cock blocked."

Dustin chuckled, but his gaze never moved from Shane's antics. "Whatever… You'll be sleeping with a new piece tonight, anyway." After a bit, he realized Todd had gone silent. He glanced over and found Todd wouldn't meet his eyes.

"Shit. You too?"

Todd glanced up. "How do you think I know lovesick when I see it?"

"Oh my God. Pussy-hound Todd falls for a girl."

A cheer erupted from the crowd and he realized they'd turned a bull loose in the arena for the bullfighters to clown with. He'd seen the entertainment before and thought it was cool. Any bull rider with a working brain respected the bullfighters. They'd saved his bacon enough times. After being with Shane, his appreciation of bullfighters had grown even more. The fear of something happening to the man he'd fallen in love with left him with a hollowness in his gut. *Fallen in love. Could anything sound so stupid and be so good?*

The show continued for several minutes. Dustin tensed as they set up the finale. Shane had talked to him about it, but he'd never seen it done. The bull twisted and ran right at Shane. Shane stuck his fingers on his head like horns, kicked up dirt with one foot then ran at the bull. *Oh, goddamn!* Dustin's hand tightened on the fence and he prayed there would be no problems.

At the last second, Shane swerved to the side then launched himself at the bull. His hands landed on the bull's hump and Shane rocketed over the ton of angry beef without a scratch. He landed feet-first on the other side and the crowd went nuts. Shane spun and did fist pumps in the air.

As he circled, their eyes met and Shane winked at him.

Once the contestants for bull riding began the competition, Dustin's focus was on nothing other than his ride. As his turn came closer, he settled into the chute, tightened his bull rope and pounded on his hand to set the rosin. As he prepared himself, Todd reappeared. With no exchanged words, he buckled a helmet and face guard on Dustin. He'd never worn one before, but the safety gear lent Dustin an added level of comfort that helped him settle into his old routine. He moved through long-established patterns and was soon ready. Dustin adjusted his seat a few times before giving a quick nod. The gate flew open and the long white bull exploded into the arena with Dustin clinging to his back. It raced the length of the enclosure, then snapped its body end for end, putting Dustin in one of the most vicious spins he'd ever experienced.

The world outside him and the bull became a smear of colors. Dustin's scattered focus narrowed to needle-fine. *Ride this damn bull. Nothing else matters.* His heart pounded in his ears as his body flooded with adrenaline. The roar of heightened sensitivity drove

Dustin until he moved in perfect time to each of the bull's maneuvers. He sensed the side flip coming and his muscles responded with accuracy only years of experience and confidence could provide.

With the next jump, the bull arched his back and spun again, lifting his feet from the ground. As the bull hit his apex, the timer sounded, marking the end of the eight seconds. Dustin sensed another disaster and his body responded before he could wrap his head around what had happened. By the time his mind and body joined again, he lay crumpled against the arena floor from an impact that left him stunned. His eyes refocused as he saw the flailing bull headed toward him.

Shane jolted into a dead run when he realized the bull couldn't land on his feet. Part of his mind quivered in fear, afraid the bull would roll over Dustin. If that happened, Dustin might not survive. But Shane slammed the door on his fear-racked inner adolescent and got down to business. No time for fancy jumps and dives — this was Save the Cowboy 101.

With his chest heaving, Shane covered the last few feet and snagged Dustin before he'd stopped rolling. He grabbed the edge of Dustin's protective vest, yanked back and slung the man behind him. The toss strained every muscle of his body. When he uncoiled from the Herculean effort, Shane found his vision filled with the slashing hooves of a massive bull.

The impact of a hoof slamming into his side crushed Shane against the ground, even as he swerved to avoid the animal. A groan of pain ripped from him when he hit the hard arena floor. Through the agony, Shane became aware of the bull moving away. Shane struggled to stand. As he did, a far too familiar pain shot through his midsection. He moved to talk to the barrelman and glimpsed Dustin being helped out of the arena by the other bullfighter.

"Hey, I gotta tape my ribs," Shane yelled.

The barrelman nodded and motioned Shane to go. "We'll stall. Go get 'em taken care of."

Shane shuffled through the crowd and wondered how he would wrap his chest by himself. When each breath of air caused a pain to shoot through his body, he realized he had broken ribs. *I should know what they're like. I've messed up enough of them.* He would work out a way to do it alone. It wouldn't be great, but it would be better than nothing. He rounded the final obstacle to the trailer to discover Dustin had arrived first. Shane couldn't believe Dustin had escaped the ride with nothing more serious than a few scrapes and a thick coating of dirt.

"Hey. What the hell are—?" Shane started.

"Where're the wraps? We need to get those ribs strapped down before they shift."

Shane pointed to the cooking area of the camper. The easily addled Dustin was focused and no-nonsense. He ripped through the contents of their kitchen and found the rolls of medical wraps. He sprinted back to Shane, his spurs whining as his feet snapped back and forth. Dustin stopped and shot Shane a dark glare.

"Well? Get your shirt off. I can't put this on over everything else. It won't do any good."

Shane stood with his mouth open and his mind trying to reconcile this very different Dustin. After a few seconds, Dustin let out a sigh of exasperation, slammed the wrap on the roof of the camper and unbuttoned

Shane's shirt. Shane woke from his daze and pushed Dustin's hands away.

"Damn it. I can undress myself," he barked.

"Then do it!"

Shane opened the last buttons and eased off his shirt until he stood bare-chested.

"Lift your arms, unless you want me to strap 'em to your sides," Dustin ordered.

Shane stuck his arms into the air and grimaced in pain as his chest moved. A few seconds later, Shane had his fingers interlaced behind his head. He glanced at Dustin, confused by the mischievousness playing across his face.

"What?"

Dustin glanced around, then dashed in and licked one of Shane's sweaty muscles. For once, Dustin's actions had no effect. The pain wrapped Shane until no sense of pleasure could break through. But Dustin's stunt gave him a comforting feeling. This was the Dustin he'd fallen for.

Dustin shot an eyebrow upward and he smirked. "Sorry, but you were so sexy I couldn't resist." He winked at Shane. "Now, let's get you taped." Dustin wound the wrap tight around Shane's torso. Within a few minutes, he was tucking the end back under another piece of wrap.

"There, that should hold you."

Shane eased his shirt and costume back on. "Get me some aspirin out of the first-aid stuff."

Dustin walked back, rustled through the drawer then shook a few tablets into his palm. He walked back around to Shane and held them out. "Here."

Shane curled his lip at the sight of Dustin's grimy hands. "I thought you'd bring the bottle."

Dustin knotted his eyebrows and his lips twisted. "Are you kidding me? You think my hands are dirty? You've had your tongue up my ass, for God's sake."

Shane rolled his eyes and swallowed the two tablets without further discussion. Dustin handed Shane a bottle of pop and Shane drank a swig to wash them down.

"Okay, I need to get back. Craig can only keep them entertained for so long."

"Go back? What the hell do you mean?"

Shane turned to Dustin. "There are other ignorant cowboys to rescue."

* * * *

Shane managed the rest of the rides with a combination of painkillers and guts. By the time the last bull rider had their go, it took all his energy to make his way to the trailer. Even with Dustin's help, Shane moaned in pain as he lowered himself onto the mattress. "Shit, crawling in this tiny thing isn't easy when you have busted ribs."

Dustin helped Shane get out of the bullfighter outfit and eased off his shirt. Unwinding the tape left Shane breathless from the agony. Dustin made a careful inspection of his side and grimaced at the deep purple bruise covering most of it.

"That's bad. Do you need to go to the hospital?" Dustin asked.

Shane craned his neck to see his side then laid back and closed his eyes. "No, it's been worse. I've cracked a few ribs. If I can keep from getting hit in the side again, I'll be fine in a few weeks."

Dustin stared at the bruise extending from under his arm to his waist. He reached out to touch it then said, "It's all hot, too."

Shane opened one eye a crack and saw Dustin hovering to see what needed to be done. Shane eased his head back down and closed his eyes again as he tried to let Dustin off the hook. "You can go to the bar with your friend if you want. You don't have to stay here and babysit me."

Dustin swung his hand toward Shane's side but stopped just short of contact and dropped it. "Don't be an asshole. I'm not used to taking care of someone else. I'm doing the best I can."

"No, I just didn't want you to think you're stuck here. I mean, we said no sleeping around, but you don't have to sit and watch me sleep."

Dustin twisted his brows together. "Why wouldn't I? I watch you sleep all the time."

Shane started at Dustin's admission. "You do?"

Dustin replied, "Yeah, I can't sleep sometimes, so I watch you sleep. When you relax, all the frowning goes away. It's kinda cool."

Shane crinkled his eyebrows. "You sit and watch me?"

"Yeah…" Dustin said with a note of concern in his voice. "Are you mad at me? Sometimes I do weird shit and don't get that it'll piss people off."

"No, not at all. I just don't get it."

Dustin wiggled close and kissed him. "You don't have to understand. I like it. I'll like it even more now when I can see you better."

Shane shook his head at Dustin then cringed and grabbed his side. "Okay, if that's what you want. I'm too sore to argue with you. But I'm gonna get some sleep."

Shane smiled as Dustin folded his legs under his butt and leaned against the wall of the camper.

Later that night, Shane drifted awake, the trailer dark now and cooler. Dustin had put a blanket over him at some point. He inhaled slowly, relieved to find the pain had decreased from excruciating to only damn painful. Glancing around the tiny enclosure, he was disappointed to find Dustin gone.

Shane gritted his teeth and pushed upward. He struggled to his elbows and scanned the trailer for a note or something. Sweat broke out on his forehead as he fought to sit upright. He shoved himself against the wall, panting as the pain crested, then receded. *Okay, the aspirin is around here somewhere. I'll take some and rest for a few minutes. I need to get started to the next rodeo. I'm sure Dustin's lost interest now that I'm pretty much helpless.*

Shane stirred, trying to use the muscles in his torso as little as possible. The door popped open and a familiar face appeared. "Hey. Cool, you're up. I walked down to a fast-food joint and grabbed us a few burgers. You hungry?"

Shane's stomach answered for him with a loud growl. "Yeah, apparently I am."

By the time he'd finished the meal, Dustin had the trailer ready to go. He'd even managed to hook up the camper without Shane knowing what had happened. Then he appeared at the door wearing a huge smile.

"Everything's ready to go. We can head out."

Shane hesitated and Dustin cocked an eyebrow. "Don't even argue with me. There's no way you can drive, all busted up like you are."

Shane thought about arguing his point but pain lanced through him when he made a slight shift. That made the decision easy. He let Dustin help him into the truck.

Shane questioned his sanity as he stared at Dustin behind the wheel of his pickup, speeding down the interstate. *But Dustin was right. No way could I have driven.* He believed his ribs had been cracked by the bull instead of broken and bruised muscles had caused most of his pain. He unbuckled the seatbelt and eased his shirt up to examine his side.

New shades of bruising added tints of yellow and red to the massive purple coloration. He worked his fingers down and pushed into his side. He hit a tender spot and sucked in his breath.

"Bad?"

He glanced across the pickup to find Dustin studying him. "Watch the road, not me." He inhaled until the pain made him stop. "Yeah, it's still sore. I need to wrap it again tonight."

Dustin's expression dropped into a scowl. "You said wrapping wasn't good for it, for you."

"And how's your side, Mister Bull Rider?"

Dustin dropped his hand to his ribs. "It's fine. I can ride."

"Yeah, well, I have to do my job, too. I'll tape it, take shit for the pain and cowboy up."

Dustin's fingers flexed around the wheel, his knuckles white. "Whatever. I was just thinking it wouldn't be a great idea."

The pain-filled day had worn on Shane, and with the battle he was having with himself over letting someone help him, it all became too much. He snapped. He twisted, pain contorting his face, and shouted, "No! It's fucking stupid! But I have to take care of myself. No one else will do a damn thing for me. I'm used to it. I've done it my whole adult life. I keep my mouth shut and my personal life under wraps. That's how I've survived in a business that hates who I am so much. It's not fucking fair, but that's how life is. So I'll suck it up, take care of myself and keep my nose clean."

Dustin glared at Shane, his lips closing to a thin line as his eyebrows twisted together. He locked his gaze on the highway, a slight tremble in his hands. "Yeah. Sure. Whatever."

Shane could almost taste the tension in the pickup.

Chapter Eleven

Shane scanned the crowd, searching for the familiar faces. They were here. It would help if they had told him who all was coming. Guilt nagged at him over how he'd blown up at Dustin. The cowboy hadn't deserved it. Shane had been exhausted, wrapped in pain and worried about their relationship. He was afraid at some point Dustin would realize he could do better and the romantic interlude would be over.

To top off the mess, Shane's family was meeting him. That was who he was trying to spot. After his last trip home, he'd had a glimmer of hope that life might cut him a break. But if he introduced Dustin to his family — to his mother, who weighed everything on her biblical scales — the carefully constructed reconciliation might come crashing down. Maybe Sam would keep up a front until he got what he wanted. Okay…Sara. Sara would always be at his side. Well, he hoped. She was young. She might decide he was wrong, too. *Oh God, why can't my life be simple?* His wallowing in pity ended when a girl jumped into his arms and wrapped her legs around his waist. The enthusiastic welcome was followed by a searing pain that doubled him over, spilling him and Sara to the ground.

Shane gritted his teeth. "Hey, Sara. Less enthusiasm would have been good."

A thick hand appeared in Shane's watery vision. He followed it upward to Sam's drawn face. "Come on. Suck it up."

Shane let out a snort of laughter, followed with another grimace of pain. "Don't make me laugh. It hurts too much. And if it was sucked up any more, I'd be a girl."

Sara popped him across the shoulder. "Hey! There's nothing wrong with being a girl. I bet I get more guys than you do!"

Shane gave Sam a bemused expression. "Please, oh please, tell me our parents have not let our little sister date."

Sam jiggled the hand he was still holding out. "You keep sitting there and you can talk to them about it."

Shane slammed his hand into his brother's, ground his teeth then shoved himself off the walkway. He regained his feet, staggered for a minute then focused on his siblings, one arm against his ribs. "So, Mom and Dad are here?"

"Sure, I texted you we were all coming!" said Sara.

He patted his sister's shoulder. "I know, I know. You and the darn texting. But sometimes plans change."

"Well, there are only the five of us," said Sara.

Shane shrugged, deciding five members in his family was more than enough. "Sounds good. Hey, I gotta get ready. I'll catch you after the bull riding."

"What are you talking about? You can't be going to bullfight with busted-up ribs," Sam said.

Shane let out a long sigh, wondering how many people would tell him what he had to do today. "I have to do it, Sam. Mesquite's huge for me to get votes."

"You're an idiot. What if one of the crazy bulls hits you again? You might get messed up and not recover."

"Not gonna happen. I'm that good."

Sam glanced toward his sister and motioned her away with a flip of his cap. "Go find Mom and Dad, will you? I need to chat with our brother."

Sara shot him a defiant glare. Sam flicked an eyebrow up his forehead. His reward was a scowl that said plainly that there would be payback before she disappeared into the crowd. Sam turned back with a dangerous expression on his face. "Look, dumb-ass. I don't care what you think, but I need you alive to do this whole new-baby thing. And I'd prefer that I didn't get the stuff from someone in a coma because they're too stupid to stay out of the arena when they're injured." He continued, "Don't get me wrong. I'd do it. But I'd rather you kinda understand what's going on."

Shane scowled back for a long minute before speaking. "So, you'd collect me like a prize bull."

"Yup, if that's what it takes."

The edge of Shane's mouth twitched. "Sounds kinda cold."

"Nah, we'd warm up the probe."

"Asshole!"

"I can be. Hey. I have an idea. Let me fill in for you, okay? No one will catch on. We're identical twins. With the makeup on, no one will be able to tell. You can get another week to nurse those ribs."

Shane shook his head. "No. Sorry, Sam. I have to do this. I appreciate the offer. But if I get this, I want it to be on my own — no cut corners, no shady deals, nothing like that."

Shane got his pain under control. Once he'd managed that feat, he glanced at his brother. "But if it'll make you happy, we can go to a sperm bank and I'll leave a deposit. Then you can keep your nasty electroejaculator out of my butt."

Sam hugged Shane.

"Ribs. Ribs!" Shane squealed.

Sam released him but kept his hands tight on Shane's biceps. "Come on. I'll help you get taped. But so help me, if you get messed up, I'll kick your ass."

"Fair enough."

They turned to leave, but some commotion the next aisle over caught Shane's attention. Someone was charging through the crowd. *Dustin?*

Shane wondered where Dustin had gone. He'd left to get soft drinks a few minutes before Sam and Sara had showed up. As soon as he got Sam settled, he headed for the trailer to make certain Dustin was all right. As he got closer, he heard a commotion there. He stepped around the corner to find Dustin and a pile of his clothes.

"Hey! Dustin! What're you doing?"

Dustin glanced up, a heart-rending expression on his face. "Getting my shit together. Gotta find Todd for a ride, but I'll be outta here soon."

Icy shock ran through Shane's system. "What's wrong? Why are you leaving?"

Dustin gave Shane a fierce glare. "I may be not too bright, but I can tell when my time's up. I don't wanna be the guy who doesn't know when he needs to get his shit and leave."

"What the hell are you talking about? Wait, wait." Shane grabbed Dustin's hands. "Wait! What's got you so pissed?"

Dustin jerked loose and wiped his arm across his face. "I saw you, okay? I get it. He's a sexy dude. I'm just a skinny kid."

Confusion and panic flooded Shane. "What the hell are you talking about? What guy?"

"Over by the chutes, you were talking to him. I went to get us something to drink and caught you in a lip lock with him when I came back. I get that I'm a lot to deal with. I'll just get the rest of my shit and —"

Shane grabbed Dustin's face and pinned it between his hands. Dustin's blue eyes darted like minnows in a shallow pool. His gaze was everywhere but on Shane. "Dustin, look at me."

Dustin slowed his frantic eye motion. He paused then met Shane's stare. Shane watched Dustin until he was certain he was listening. "A guy about my height, a little skinnier, same hair, basically the spitting image of me?"

Dustin's Adam's apple jumped as he swallowed, then he gave a slight nod.

"And you've been getting all pissed off since you saw him — right?"

Dustin gulped again. "Yeah, well. It all seemed cozy. It was a hot kiss."

Shane ran his thumbs over Dustin's lashes and the almost imperceptible moisture clinging to them. "First, ick! That was my twin brother, Sam, and there was no kiss. My family came to see me. Sara, my sister, was there, too. Tall, gangly teenager."

Dustin shrugged, but some of the tension bled out of his body. "Really? No shitting me?"

"Really. No shitting you." Shane released Dustin.

Concern flashed on Dustin's face. "Do you need me to leave? You know, keep us secret?"

Shane let out a long sigh. "I've been trying to figure that out all day, too. For the first time in a long time, my family and I are getting along—partly because Sam asked for a favor and I said I would help, partly because Sara's on my side and tells our parents how wrong they are all the time." He admired his sister's tenacity. *If I were as strong as her, this wouldn't even be a question.*

When Shane saw Dustin's hurt expression, the whole issue became black and white. Regardless of how tense his relationship with his family had gotten, they'd never thrown him out. They'd always said they loved him. But Dustin hadn't been that fortunate, and now Shane had considered asking him to hide their relationship. Shane was ashamed of himself.

"No, I don't want you to leave or anything. I'd like for you to come meet my family. They'll like you." A sudden thought stopped Shane. "Ah, there is one thing."

Dustin nodded, seeming to brace himself. "Yeah?"

"My mom's very religious. Like bible-up-her-butt religious."

Dustin nodded.

"Could you keep the cussing down to a minimum, like none?"

Dustin let out a breath. "Sure. Well, I'll try."

"If you don't, you'll get 'the look' at best, and fire-and-brimstone preaching at worst."

"I've gotten the fire and brimstone enough times, but I'll try hard to be good."

Shane hauled the slender cowboy against him, pressed his lips against his forehead and whispered, "You already are good. Never forget that."

Dustin hugged him tight and pain shot through Shane. He winced as the agony of his ribs filled him.

Dustin recoiled, concern written across his face. "What's wrong?"

"Well, my ribs haven't miraculously healed. What'd you think was wrong?"

"Oh, shoot. What can I do to help?"

"Help me get ready to go out. Sam agreed to tape me up, but I'd just as soon you do it. If you're wrapping my ribs, you'll be careful because I'll get even."

"Okay, no problem. I know how to tape someone, I've had it done enough. And I'll be careful. It seems like one or the other of us needs it all the time. I don't want you thumping me sometime later."

"That'd be great. Then, afterward, you can meet the Reeses. We're a fun bunch."

Dustin stared at Shane, cocked his eyebrow then set to work without comment.

* * * *

A bit later they sat in the pickup outside the hotel Shane's parents had picked, hoping this wasn't a mistake. Once Shane had decided, he'd been at peace with it, but Dustin was a bundle of nerves. Shane knew Dustin's backstory and hated to put him through the turmoil of dealing with his family, too. Family issues had kept his boyfriend's life ripped to shreds for years.

Shane grabbed Dustin's thigh and squeezed it. "Come on. Sara will check constantly, and when she sees us, all hell will break loose."

He wiped his sweaty hands on his pressed Wranglers again then swung his legs out of the pickup and took the slight hop needed to hit the ground. They had almost reached the door when it burst open like a roping gate. A high-pitched squeal assaulted his ears.

"Shane!"

Sara grabbed him in a tight hug. He let out a grunt of pain but still held on to her.

After a few seconds, she let go and caught Dustin. "Hey, I'm Shane's sister, Sara, in case you haven't figured it out."

"Hey, I'm Dustin Lewis. I'm Shane's — "

Dustin glanced at Shane and he knew Dustin didn't want to be the one to deliver the news to his family.

"He's my boyfriend. Don't ask what he sees in me, but he keeps sticking around."

Sara winked at Dustin. "Isn't it cute when they don't even realize how hot they are?"

Anxiety and delight flooded Shane at Sara's enthusiasm, but he recognized an ally when he saw one and leaned in close to Sara. "Dustin would be the cute one. It comes from being the one riding the bull instead of the one being chased by it."

Sara laughed, a melodic sound that matched her. "Big brother, you don't pick occupations very well."

Dustin winked at her. "That's what I keep telling him, too."

The interplay stopped when someone cleared their throat. They glanced back to find the guy Dustin had seen hugging him earlier. "You three wanna bring it inside or do we need to divide up teams for flag football?"

Sara let out a very unladylike snort. "Flag football is for wimps. If I'm gonna play, it's gonna be tackle."

"And that's why half the boys at school are afraid of you, Sara." A short sturdy woman pushed her way through the family. "All of you, get inside. My goodness, the children I've raised have spent far too much time in barns."

"Come on, kids. You heard your mom." The newest arrival stuck out his hand to Dustin. "I'm Matt, Shane's dad. Good to meet you, Dustin."

Shane could tell that his dad's acceptance was a new experience for his father. Dustin followed the rest of the family inside. Once they were in the room, everyone spread out onto chairs, couches and beds. Shane took Dustin by the arm, guided him to the couch and sat beside him. Dustin patted Shane's hand.

"Hello, Dustin. My name's Laura. I'm sure you've figured out I'm Shane's mother."

"Yes, ma'am, I did. I'm pleased to meet you, ma'am."

"Yes, it's nice to meet you, too. I like to meet the people my children are with." Her eyebrows lifted as she caught Shane's gaze. "Even when they don't tell me they're with someone."

Shane squirmed in his seat, his stomach in knots as he stared at the floor. "Sorry, Mom."

She lifted an eyebrow then turned back to Shane. "How long have you two been dating?"

"A few months," said Shane.

"A month," said Dustin at the same time.

Laura laughed and the tension in the room slipped away. "So, for a while. Well, I don't want you to think I'm quizzing you. It's time to get food." She turned to her husband. "Matt, you taking us to Saltgrass?"

"Yes, hon. You love the steaks there."

Laura winked at Dustin. "They think I don't understand they take me there to soften me up for something. Wonder what they think I need softening up about this time?" She laughed as the family made their way out of the hotel room.

Shane followed everyone to the restaurant, thinking it would give them some breathing space.

"I think that went well. But I might not be the best judge." Dustin said.

Shane smiled. "So far so good. I'm hoping it will keep going this good."

Dustin nodded and leaned back into the seat. "Yeah, right."

Shane's wishful prediction was coming true as he shared a piece of chocolate cake with Dustin. The meal had been quiet as everyone ordered their favorites and fell on them like starving wolves. At least there'd been no shit grenades lobbed at them. Dustin was keeping his hyperactivity under wraps, too. Shane was a little guilty that Dustin felt the need to act different. Dustin had made sure Shane saw him take his medication before they'd left the trailer. Shane didn't understand what it did for Dustin and he didn't want his boyfriend to feel like he had to be drugged for Shane to be around him, but it did seem to help him control what he said and did.

Shane lifted the bite of cake and slipped it in his mouth. In spite of the Adderall Dustin had taken, he was still bouncing his leg like crazy. In an attempt to relax him, Shane slid his hand over Dustin's and squeezed. His reward was a quick smile.

"That was delicious, as always," said Laura.

Shane's focus shifted to his mother, knowing this would be the make-it-or-break-it maneuver.

"But y'all wasted your money on the bribe part."

Concern and confusion flashed around the table.

"It was delicious, though." Laura grinned at Dustin. "See, Dustin. They expected me to throw a hissy fit about you and Shane being together." She held up her hand, appearing to want to forestall any potential arguments. "I didn't handle it well when Shane first told us. And I haven't told him this, but I should have." She met Shane's eyes with a slight wetness around her own. "Son, I'm ashamed of myself for how I treated you. I've done a lot of praying and a lot of talking to people who should understand the bible." She inhaled deeply. "This should be easy, but I guess faith is never easy if you want to decide what it says. I've changed, Shane. I don't have all the answers. But I want my son to be happy, and if Dustin makes you happy then you have my blessing."

Shane collapsed into his chair, feeling as though a weight had been lifted from him. Unable to control himself, he flung his arms around Dustin and kissed him until there were groans from the table.

"Jeez! Get a room!" Sam waved them away, beaming the whole time.

Sara reached over and nudged Shane. "Ah, big brother. The 'rents are still at the table."

Dustin struggled to pull away and Shane released him from the kiss. The fear and apprehension on his face shouted that he expected the world to open and swallow him. But Shane held his gaze with a serene smile and that seemed to calm him.

"This is crazy…" Dustin finally said.

Shane laughed and leaned his forehead against Dustin's as relief washed over him. He glanced around the table to a sea of happy faces. When he met eyes with his mother, long-absent understanding passed between them.

I won't soon forget tonight.

Chapter Twelve

Something was wrong. Dustin couldn't put his finger on it, but he had the same sensation he got before a big storm. He tugged the sheet over them and pressed himself against Shane. Shane made the tiny snort he always made when he woke up and his being awake seemed like the best remedy for Dustin's sense of impending disaster. Shane usually made everything all right—at least in his world. Today, he wasn't able to shake his concern as Shane rolled toward him and held them tightly against each other.

"What's up?" Shane asked in a morning grumble.

"Just still nervous."

Shane stretched, his arms almost touching the sides of the trailer as he did. Dustin loved Shane's muscles coiling and uncoiling beneath his head. When the stretch ended, Shane curled his muscular arms around Dustin, who found himself back in a warm hug. Surrounded by Shane's tight embrace, Dustin felt safe. He leaned in and kissed Shane's rough cheek.

"I'm usually right about these kinds of things. Something will go wrong."

Shane brushed his fingers along Dustin's back. "You've been fretting since we got to Greeley. What's up? I don't see any problem. Tonight's the last round, and we'll leave."

Dustin threw up his hands in exasperation. "I can't figure out why I feel like this. It seems as though we're being watched, like something's about to happen. There were those townies who kept staring at us. What about them?"

"You're a worrywart. You need to stop watching all those werewolf shows, then you won't have nightmares."

Dustin elbowed Shane in the ribs, getting a sharp grunt of pain in response. "Sorry. Forgot the ribs are still kinda touchy. But don't mess with my intuition. I'm telling you, something's coming and we're not gonna like it."

Shane drew Dustin tighter, leaned in and nibbled on his ear. "Babe, you need to relax. Life is good for once. My family likes you. Sara loves you. You're just not used to things going right."

Dustin shuddered as Shane kissed down his neck. "Stop it. You're not going to distract me. I tell you—Ohhh…"

Shane flicked his tongue across Dustin's nipple a few more times before they kissed again. "You still want to worry or do you want to play?"

Shane slid his fingers down Dustin's chest then into his pubes. The tug on them made his worries dissolve into nothing. "Harder. More."

Dustin rolled his eyes at Shane's next maneuver and soon forgot the conversation.

* * * *

Dustin was at the trailer, still enjoying the after-hot-sex glow while getting ready, when his phone went off. 'Todd's Parents' flashed across his screen and he answered the call. "Hey…"

"Hi, Dustin. It's Todd's dad."

"Yeah, hi. What's going on?"

"I checked out your pickup. It's pretty well shot."

"That bad, huh?"

"Yeah, not much I can do to patch the problems this time. It'll take a couple thousand bucks to fix it."

"Really? Wow. I don't have that kind of money."

Shane stopped applying the clown makeup, his face a portrait of concern as he stared at Dustin.

"Okay, Mr. Martin. What should I do?"

"Do you have a way to get to the rest of the rodeos?"

Dustin's gaze flicked to Shane. "Yeah, I'm pretty sure I can get that done."

"If you win enough this fall, we can talk about making repairs. I'll park it out back until you decide what you want to do," Todd's father said,

"Okay. Take good care of her, please. She's kind of important."

"It'll be fine, Dustin. Nothing will happen to your truck."

"That's good. Well, I better go. My round's coming up," he said.

"Tell Todd good luck from us. You be sure and be careful, too, Dustin."

"Yeah, I'll be sure and do that."

"Okay, take care."

"You, too." Dustin sat staring at the phone, lost in thought.

"Well?" Shane asked.

Dustin glanced at him with a solemn expression. "It'll be okay. He'll take care of her."

"Her who? Him who? What the hell's going on? Is everyone okay?"

Surprise washed over Dustin, then he realized Shane had only gotten his side of the conversation. "Everything's fine. 'She' is my pickup. That was Todd's dad telling me how much it would cost to fix her."

Relief washed through Shane. "Your pickup! Well, shit! I was afraid someone got hurt."

Dustin shook his head. "Nope, but she's important. I left home in her and slept a lot of nights in the bed when I didn't have money for a room."

Shane nodded. "Yeah, I get that. So what are you going to do?"

"Well"—a flush of heat slid up Dustin's face—"I hoped you'd be willing to let me keep traveling with you—"

Shane popped Dustin on the shoulder. "Of course, dumb-ass. I like having my boyfriend with me."

Dustin thought he caught movement from the corner of his eye, but when he checked the area around their campsite, he didn't find anything. He shifted his gaze back to Shane and winked. "Me, too. Never had a boyfriend before."

Shane returned the wink and went back to putting on his makeup. A moment later Shane's movements slowed and he turned to Dustin. "Hey, this was your bad thing. What you were worried about. Your pickup breaking down and not being fixable... That was the stuff that's been worrying you."

Dustin considered the possibility for a minute then shrugged. "Might be. That would explain a few things.

I'd sure be happy if the whole thing was just my pickup."

Shane dropped the makeup sponge into his box. "It is. Now you can stop worrying."

Dustin fastened the last buckle on his chaps, stood and stomped his feet to make sure everything was nice and snug. "Okay, well, I'm ready."

Shane tossed the last of his equipment into the trailer and locked the door. "Me, too. I'll go save your ass again tonight."

Dustin glanced at him with humor-filled eyes and blew him a raspberry before they headed toward the arena.

* * * *

Shane wasn't clear from Dustin's directions where they were meeting. He'd found Dustin's note on the trailer door when he came back to clean up after the last event for the afternoon. It hadn't seemed too unusual until he wandered into a deserted part of the fairgrounds. The fading sunlight made it difficult to see. This was where all the crap they didn't know what to do with came to die.

Why in the hell would Dustin want to meet here? *If this is for some time to mess around, I'll be pissed. This is ridiculous.* Shane jumped when something shot across the ground. He calmed when the tip of a rat's tail disappeared as it scurried under another pile. The mounds of junk grew as he wandered deeper inside until only narrow trails snaked between them. Shane worried as the light slipped away.

"Hey! Dustin! Where the hell are you?" he yelled.

Silence met his call. There wasn't even a comforting echo as the piles absorbed his voice.

I don't like this.

Shane turned to leave when something hit him from behind and he was knocked face-first into the gravel. The weight crushing down on him left Shane breathless. His vision narrowed when air refused to enter his lungs. He was pushing himself from the ground when a kick delivered by a heavy boot landed in his ribs, the dizzying pain overwhelming him as his healing ribs felt as though they'd broken again.

"Stay put, you fucking fag! We're gonna make sure you never come back to Greeley again."

Shane realized what was happening and struggled to escape. His efforts earned him another vicious kick. This one hit more stomach than ribs, for which Shane was thankful, but the work boot to his gut still folded him in half. He tried to get up to crawl on his hands and knees, but his body was responding as if he were moving through cold molasses. He stopped, his head spinning from shock and blinding pain, then he collapsed.

"Get him up, guys. Worthless queers like him shouldn't be alive."

Shane wanted to curl into a misery-filled ball to contain the agony. The two silent attackers jerked him up. They held him immobile, one on each arm. Shane tried to fight back when a hand grabbed his hair and yanked his head backward.

"We're gonna fuck you up! When we're done with you, you won't have a dick left for your sick boyfriend." Shane struggled as his fear built that they'd already jumped Dustin. He tried to stand, but his body refused to cooperate. He wished he'd put more credence in Dustin's 'feelings'.

Shane squinted to see the attacker's face, trying to place his torturer and failing. *Someone I've never met will kill me for being gay.*

The lunatic's eyes glinted as he licked his lips and formed a vile grin. "Hold him still. I'm gonna fix this faggot."

Shane saw the kick coming, but they held him so it was impossible to dodge and the boot slammed into his testicles. Unbearable pain flooded Shane's body and his stomach roiled. He crashed against the hard ground when they dropped him, the blinding pain overwhelming him as he waited to die.

* * * *

Dustin paced outside the arena as his concern built. "I'm telling you that something's wrong. Everything just feels off. I called and texted him. He doesn't answer." Dustin was so frazzled that he vibrated with nervous energy.

"Calm down. Did you take your Adderall?" Todd asked.

"Fuck you! Something's wrong."

Todd held his hands out to deflect Dustin's rage. "Okay, okay. You're right a scary amount of the time. Could it be this town? The rodeo's over. Find Shane, and we'll get the hell outta here."

Panic built in Dustin as he tried to hurry Todd. "Oh God. Something's happened to Shane. I don't know what, but something. I told you about that bunch of locals who kept staring at us." Dustin took a step then broke into a run, desperate to find his boyfriend.

Todd ran after him and yelled, "Where you headed?"

"To the trailer park down by the river."

Todd peeled away. Dustin yelled at his friend, "Where're you going?"

"For reinforcements!" Todd called out as he headed off.

Dustin turned his focus toward the race to find Shane.

He heard a strangled scream, and from somewhere, he found the energy to pick up his speed and sprint in the direction of the desperate sound. The first thing he saw when he arrived was Shane on the ground, trying to spit the dirt from his mouth while blood trickled down the side of his face from the cut above his eye.

Dustin let out an ear-shattering yell as he jumped on the closest attacker. He clenched his legs around the man and pounded the attacker's face while tightening his legs.

"Get him off! Get the motherfucker off! Ahh! He's biting my damn ear!" the attacker screamed.

Dustin continued pounding the side of the assailant's head with his fist. A bit of relief washed through him when he saw Shane stumble to his feet. When Shane picked up a fist-sized rock and moved toward them, Dustin's emotions swung from fearful that he would become injured more severely than he already was to proud that after being beaten, Shane still continued to fight.

A shrill cry of pain filled the air and broke Dustin's concentration. His attention flickered toward the noise and his concern was replaced with a smile of grim determination when he saw Shane using the rock against the man who'd attacked him. Shane seemed to have found new resolve to fight back. Dustin's focus returned to the thug he'd jumped. He landed his fists like a high plains hailstorm and started to have an effect.

His resolve faltered at the sound of wood against muscle punctuated by a piercing scream. *Shit! They found a board to use.* With the second sound of a weapon against flesh, Dustin locked down his emotions and turned to either rescue Shane or go down fighting. But the scene around him was not what he'd expected. Standing beside Shane, swinging a baseball bat like it was Excalibur, was Todd and a couple of other guys from the rodeo were running toward them. Their combined efforts soon had the assailants backing away with each step.

Dustin spun at the sound of someone charging him. The years of judo as a kid kicked in. He found his sense of calm and waited. When the expected assault materialized, he grabbed the wrist in a vise-like grip and dropped to a single knee. The attacker arched over Dustin to land face-first several feet in front of him. There was an instant of quiet before the ringleader scrambled through the gravel to propel himself toward escape and yelled at the other two, "Get outta here!"

"Chicken-shit cowards!" Todd screamed as they scrambled away. He turned and quickly checked Dustin's injuries then turned to Shane. The other cowboys gave chase.

Dustin was surprised when Shane grabbed Todd's hands. Dustin was concerned about the expression of worry Shane shot toward his friend, but Shane's next words clarified everything. "Hang on, Todd. There's blood everywhere. You need to be careful. I'm fine. I've been tested recently, but there is a lot of blood."

Todd didn't hesitate before checking Shane over. "It's not like I carry rubber gloves like they were condoms.

Seems like most of the blood is yours. I sure wasn't going to avoid helping Dustin's boyfriend, regardless of how much you're bleeding."

Shane froze, shocked. His gaze flicked back to Todd, who shrugged and resumed checking Shane's injuries. He spent several minutes going over Shane as Dustin hovered nearby. Once he seemed satisfied, Todd motioned toward Dustin. "My family isn't as dumb as Dustin thinks. We've always known. But we figured it was Dustin's secret to keep or his to tell. He finally told me a while back."

Todd focused on Dustin. "We need an ambulance here, but I think it would be faster to put the two of you in the bed of my truck instead of waiting."

Dustin assessed the amount of blood coating Shane and nodded in agreement. "Okay, but we need to go now."

Todd said, "I'm going for my pickup to take you to the ER." He turned to Dustin. "Get him to the edge of all this crap but be careful. He probably has something broken."

He nodded toward Shane. "You're going to need stitches. Your face is all kinds of fucked up."

"My face was fucked up already. Don't worry about it," Shane said with resignation.

* * * *

Dustin sat on the examination table with his feet in nonstop motion. The doctor had stitched up a cut he'd gotten on his face and he was waiting to be released. He was worried about Shane. Todd had been back and forth between their rooms and said he was fine. He also said a cop was questioning him. Dustin didn't care what had happened to their attackers, although he figured they'd end up at the hospital at some point, too. Todd wielded a pretty mean bat. But right now Dustin was focusing on how bad a shape Shane had been in by the time they'd reached the ER.

The curtain skittered back and the physician's assistant who'd been fixing him up walked in with a clipboard. "Just a few things to wrap up. Here's a couple of prescriptions — one for the pain if you need something, the other for antibiotic cream that's stronger than what you can get over the counter."

Dustin tried to listen as the physician's assistant covered his discharge information, but he wanted to be with Shane. The PA stopped for a breath and Dustin refused to hold back any longer. "How's Shane? Is he okay? Can I see him?"

He smiled at Dustin. "He's been asking for you, too. Hang on a minute and I'll see what I can do."

Dustin nodded, trying to keep his frustration under wraps. His anxiety had become unbearable by the time the PA returned. "Okay, you can go in." Dustin jumped off the table and grimaced. He paused a second to let his body adjust then started out of the door and almost ran into the PA. "Hey, you two should think about getting married. If you were, you wouldn't have to worry about getting to check on your husband. Unmarried couples don't have too many rights. But once he asked for you, it was cool." Then the PA shrugged. "For whatever it's worth, my husband and I got married as soon as it was legal, and that was part of the reason."

Dustin barely heard him in his obsession to get to Shane. Although part of him was screaming *'Married? We're only at the dating stage.'* But he avoided any response that might slow things down. He nodded. "How do I get to Shane?"

"He's in a room. I'll take you."

Dustin followed through a series of twists and turns until he stood in front of a closed door. The PA said, "This is his room. I'll check on you in a few minutes. We want to make sure he doesn't have a concussion before we release him." He paused. "The police should be finished with him, too."

Dustin nodded. He pressed the door open, afraid of what he would find. "Shane?"

"Dustin? You okay?"

Dustin walked into the room and froze. Shane's face was a latticework of dark stitches. Both eyes were black and one was almost swollen shut. Shane seemed oblivious to the uniformed officer watching them both.

"Oh shit. They fucked you up." Dustin slapped his hand to his mouth.

"It's okay. They stitched up everything so the scars would be smaller. They said in a month or so you won't even see them."

The officer cleared his throat. "I have everything, Mr. Rees. I expect the attack will be classified a hate crime, so other agencies will be involved. We'll catch the people responsible."

"Thanks, Officer. I appreciate the help."

The cop nodded at Dustin, closed his notebook and walked out of the room. Dustin thought he showed amazing restraint by waiting until the door clicked shut before rushing to Shane. He grabbed Shane's wrapped hand and got a yelp of pain. "Oh God. Is there anywhere I can touch you and it won't hurt?"

"Try the back of my knees. They didn't hit me there. X-rays showed a couple of fingers broke. At some point the guy you jumped stomped on my hand." Shane lifted his hand and the gauze fell back, revealing a couple of metal splints.

"How is everything else? Anything serious?"

"Not really, just pretty banged up. They would have killed me if you and Todd and the others hadn't come when you did."

"I just knew they'd killed you. You were lying there and the little guy was kicking you."

Shane snorted and shook his head. "He wasn't that small. At least he didn't seem like it."

Dustin waved his hand in the air and sat on the side of Shane's bed. "Well, compared to the other two goons, he was a runt."

Shane chuckled, then gasped. "Stop it. Don't make me laugh. It hurts."

Dustin leaned in and kissed Shane on the cheek. "Sorry, babe. I'll watch my comedy routine."

Shane narrowed his swollen eyes.

"Sorry. I'm done," Dustin said.

They sat quietly for several minutes. Dustin slid his hand across the sheet and rested his fingers on the back of Shane's hand. "It'll be fine. They'll catch the bastards."

"I guess I'll have to go home for a few weeks. I'm gonna need help to get around."

Dustin's heart fell. "Oh…"

"What's wrong?" Shane asked.

"Nothing."

"What's bothering you? Don't you trust me?"

"I do. It's just me being stupid," Dustin replied.

"What?"

"Okay. Fine. It pisses me off that you don't want me to take care of you. But if you want to go home, that's okay," Dustin admitted.

Shane stared at him, his mouth hanging open until Dustin tired of waiting for his response and asked, "What? I know I'm not that bright. I get reminded every morning when I have to pop a pill to function."

"No, that's not it. I figured you'd be sick of taking care of me. You've already had to help for weeks and this is gonna be worse."

"Why wouldn't I want to take care of my boyfriend, and why would this time be different?"

"Nothing's broken, but I'm pretty banged up. I don't know if I can take care of myself."

Dustin winked at Shane. "If you mean like beat off, I'm happy to help with that."

"No, asshole. Like wiping my butt after I crap. I'm pretty sure I couldn't right now."

"So, you'd rather have your mom or Sam do it?"

Shane's face twisted, as if he was thinking of his reply, when there was a knock at the door and the doctor walked in.

"Well, Mr. Rees. How would you like to go home?"

Chapter Thirteen

The last few days had helped Shane. Mending miles of barbed-wire fence and working on the corrals had kept him from obsessing over the attack as he did when he had too much quiet time on his hands. The nightmares had even disappeared. He wiped his face with his forearm, which only smeared bits of alfalfa and dirt. Soon the hay would be too dry to bale any more today, which was fine with Shane. He was ready to stop. They'd been hauling it since before dawn. He hadn't expected this to be his relaxation during his visit, but working with his family and Dustin had played an important part in his recovery.

He glanced down from the hay wagon to see Dustin teasing Sara and heard her unfettered laughter in response. They were joshing with each other almost as much as the dogs Mutt and Jeff, who were enjoying running and bowling each other over. He was happy his boyfriend and sister were getting along. Actually, Dustin had gotten along well with everyone in his family so far. He and Sara had really bonded, though.

Shane wouldn't question his luck this time. He lurched backward as a bale of hay plowed into his leg.

"You dinking around over there?" Dustin tossed another bale toward him.

"Hey! Who had to drag your a—" Shane glanced at his sister. "Drag you out of bed."

"Nah, I was catnapping. Just needed another five minutes of sleep. Besides, I was still ready before you were."

Shane tossed the bale to the top of the stack and jammed it against the side. "Only because you slept in your jeans and didn't bother to put on a shirt." *Another reason I'm distracted.*

"That's it," Sara said. "That was the last bale, and Dad says it's too dry to put up any more today."

Shane sighed. "Good! I'm ready to clean up and take a nap. Let's get this load in the barn."

They rode through the midmorning quiet. Only the occasional call of quail punctuated their exhaustion. Sam pulled the wagon into the barn and the four of them made short work of unloading. They were putting the gear away when Sam walked over to Shane and Dustin. "Umm, I need to talk to you for a sec, bro."

Shane wasn't in the mood for Sam's jokes. He was tired and sore. "What?"

Sam glanced in Dustin's direction and back. "That deal. The one we talked about last time you were home? I need to talk with you about it."

Dustin wrinkled his eyebrows and studied first Shane then his brother. After a minute, he shrugged. "Go do your brother shit. You aren't gonna offend me."

Shane ran his hand down Dustin's back then followed Sam to his pickup and climbed inside.

"What's going on? I'm too damn tired to work out anything complicated."

Sam squirmed before blurting out, "They need a sample to check for any problems."

"Sample?"

Sam sighed. "A semen sample. The fertility clinic needs one." He handed Shane a brown sack.

Shane glanced inside then clinched the bag shut. "It's a damn good thing I'm your twin because I wouldn't do this for anybody else."

Sam threw up his hands and slumped against the seat. "I'm not enjoying these little talks either."

"Okay, well, what do I do?"

"Oh hell! I have no idea. There's a whole sheet of instructions in there."

"You are such a pain in the ass."

Sam snorted and opened his pickup door with Shane not far behind. Shane saw the curiosity on Dustin's face but didn't want to repeat the whole discussion. He was thoroughly put out about the whole mess he'd let himself get into to help Sam.

Shane walked back to Dustin with the brown paper sack wadded up in his hand. When he got close enough, Shane could see that Dustin was about to burst with laughter.

"What's in that bag to make you have that sourpuss expression on your face? Did Sam give you a turd or something?"

Shane shoved the bag at him. "Well, he kinda did. Damn brothers…"

Dustin took the bag and peeked inside. "A bag and a cup? That's it?"

"It's a specimen cup."

Dustin giggled. "You gotta pee in a cup for your brother? I woulda thought he'd pass a drug test without switching pee."

Shane shook his head. "No, not pee. The other stuff…"

Dustin shrugged.

"You know. I told you." Shane stuck his fist in front of his crotch and made jerking motions.

Dustin snickered. "Why are you jacking off for your brother?"

"No! Remember? We already talked about it. I'm the sperm donor for their baby. The clinic needs a sperm sample. They have to run tests or something."

"Yeah, I forgot that you told me. I think it's way cool for you to help your brother like that."

"Yeah, well, now I have to do this and it's embarrassing."

"Why?" Dustin asked.

"Why what?"

"Like, why are you embarrassed?"

"Because! Everyone will know I've…done it," Shane explained.

"Babe, I'm betting they already know you jerk off."

Shane popped Dustin on the back of the head. "Asshole. Not everyone's as blunt about the whole sex thing as you are."

Dustin slid closer and kissed Shane. "I can help…"

Shane's whole focus shifted at the offer. His dick stiffened the way it did each time they touched. When he heard the distant voices of his family, though, it was as though they'd dumped ice water on him. "Not now. Everyone's still here. Dammit, it's always something."

* * * *

The next day Shane glared at the sack that had been mocking him from its perch on the counter. He wasn't upset anymore about what he had to do but he was running out of time. His family had left and he had an hour or so of privacy. Dustin sat on the side of their bed while Shane paced back and forth.

"Okay, so once we do it…" Shane said.

"Beat your meat." Dustin snickered.

Shane rolled his eyes and sighed. "Collect the sample. Then we have to get it to the doctor's office in less than an hour."

"No problem. And I'll take the stuff in, if it's that big of a thing to you," Dustin offered.

"Really? Because I'd appreciate that."

Dustin kissed Shane and ran his hands down Shane's chest. "Okay, read the instructions again."

"Wash up. No lube, spit or anything else. Seal it up. Get the stuff to the office."

Dustin surveyed the RV they'd been staying in while at the ranch. "Well, that shower is tiny. I don't think I can help you in there."

Shane undressed. When his underwear hit the floor, Dustin slapped Shane's ass. "Nice piece of meat."

The slap traveled through Shane, focusing on his half-hard cock and causing it to grow. He turned on the water in the shower and wedged himself inside. Dustin watched as he lathered up. "What?"

"You've got a hot body. I can't wait to make you squirt."

Shane shook his head, but the comment made his cock swell further. "Damn, Dustin. You don't hold back."

Dustin leered at Shane while he tried to hurry. "I have the hottest boyfriend in Texas. Why wouldn't I want to have sex with you all the time?"

Shane ignored the comment as he rinsed off the last bits of soap. When he stepped back, he took the towel Dustin held out for him. He dried himself when Dustin stepped up and kissed his shoulder.

Shane reached back and ruffled Dustin's hair. "You're excited about this whole thing."

"Damn straight I am. I get to jerk you off in the middle of the day and your family is fine with it."

Embarrassment flooded Shane. "Come on, Dustin. Give me a break. They know what we're doing."

Dustin ran his hands over Shane, letting them slide lower, and he fondled Shane's balls. "Why do you care? They asked you to do this. Just relax and let me take care of things."

Dustin pushed him backward until he was against the bed. With a final shove, Shane landed in their nest of bedding. He scooted higher and propped himself on his elbows. Dustin climbed between his legs and ran his fingers along the insides of Shane's thighs. Waves of pleasure and lust ran through Shane and his cock transformed into steel.

"Man, that feels good," Shane groaned.

"We want to make sure the doc has enough to work with. I think I'll edge you for a while," Dustin said.

"What the hell is edging?" Shane asked.

He gasped as Dustin took his nipple between his teeth and nipped, sending an electric current directly to Shane's crotch. He fell back on the bed, his mind a haze as Dustin attacked his chest. After several wonderful minutes, Shane's climax built from Dustin's erotic dance with his nipples. His lust and love were mounting when Dustin stopped.

Shane crawled back to his elbows, panting hard. "Why'd you stop?"

"You were about to come. That sorta fucks with the whole idea of edging, now doesn't it? And I bet you know what edging is now, too."

Shane dropped back to the bed, his breath still coming in gasps. *Edging, fuck. We're having a discussion about this...after he's done.* He closed his eyes to enjoy the sensations but sprang them open when Dustin smashed warm, moist lips against his. Shane opened his mouth a crack at the insistent burrowing of Dustin's tongue. He slipped inside Shane's mouth and kissed him passionately for several minutes, with sharp pleasure washing over Shane before Dustin broke the embrace. Shane shuddered as he gasped for air. "Stop doing that!"

Dustin traced his fingers over Shane's torso. "I want you good and horned up when we go for it." With that, Dustin showed that he'd paid more attention to the porn they sometimes watched together than Shane had thought. He repeatedly hit each of Shane's erogenous zones. Dustin explored again and again until Shane's body was aflame with desire. Dustin gripped his cock and Shane tried to focus on the reason for the afternoon fun.

"Close. God. Remember."

Dustin jammed his thumb against the underside of Shane's cock, sending a final jolt of fire through his system. He moaned as the first shot released from deep inside him. The pleasure was sweet after the long buildup and Shane shot again and again. As his body emptied, he panicked.

"Shit, I forgot—"

Dustin smirked and held up a small container, now sealed and half-full of ivory-colored cream. "You mean this?"

Shane let himself enjoy the afterglow. Dustin moved off the bed to set the sample inside the bag. Shane could see from the tent in front of Dustin's crotch that he hadn't been immune to the foreplay, either. "Come on. Let me take care of you."

Dustin shook his head. "Get dressed. This stuff has a shelf life."

He crawled to the edge of the bed and grabbed Dustin's crotch. "I'll thrill you later."

Dustin grinned at him and slapped his bare butt. "Get up, slug. We gotta go!"

Dropping off the semen sample wasn't the drama Shane had feared. The office was very professional about the whole thing. But, as Dustin pointed out, that was pretty much what they did all day long, so it hadn't even rated the random blink.

* * * *

A few days later the package Shane had been waiting for arrived. As with everything else, his family had excelled at being cock blockers. But after a few days, the perfect opportunity to spring his surprise on Dustin presented itself. Dustin hadn't gotten off for days, which would make it that much sweeter. Shane had planned the seduction for a day his family would be in Amarillo—not that it would take much to seduce Dustin. Shane wanted their time together to be something more than clothes ripping and butt banging, although that would be part of the fun. His attachment to and budding feelings for Dustin had grown more tangible during their visit to his parents. He'd packed the two of them a picnic lunch and planned to take Dustin out to a secluded spot he knew. His first thought had been a horseback ride, but then he remembered Dustin had never ridden a horse. He took the ranch Jeep instead. He settled the plastic cooler with their meal inside the vehicle and went to the RV to collect Dustin.

Shane stuck his head inside to find him asleep, with an erection. Unable to resist, Shane grabbed Dustin's crotch to awaken him. "Come on, stud. I have something planned for us."

Dustin let out a murmur and clasped his hands over Shane's. "Keep doing that. I'm so horny. Someone in your family is always around and checking on us."

"Well, get your ass out of bed, because they're gone today."

Dustin popped up. "No shit?"

"No shit. Now get up and let's go. I have the Jeep packed already. I thought we'd take advantage of the time alone."

Dustin bounded up, slung his arms into the sleeves of his shirt and rammed his socked feet into his worn boots. As he raced to the door, he grabbed Shane, kissed him hard then tugged him to the waiting vehicle. "Come on! Let's get going. Your damn family is liable to change their mind and come back early."

"Okay, okay. Let's go. Everything's packed."

Dustin vaulted into the Jeep and held on to the roll bar as Shane took off. The wind caught Dustin's shirt and blew it open. He loved Dustin's taut body. He wanted to stop, take him down and trace his fingers through the faint muscular curve that ran down his sides to plunge into his jeans. *No question about it, Dustin is sexy. If only I could trust that he has feelings for me.* It still surprised him how much the rest of his family liked Dustin.

Shane refocused on his driving as they crested a ridge and plummeted down the steep bank. He couldn't help but laugh as Dustin yelped at the exhilaration of the ride. The minute they stopped, Dustin climbed into his lap.

"Fuck me! I need it!"

Shane laughed as Dustin attacked him like a hen after a grasshopper. "Don't you want to eat first?"

"Eat. Later. Fuck. Now," Dustin said with a kiss between each word.

"Okay, but there's one thing first."

Dustin groaned. "What? I wanna fuck!"

Shane pushed Dustin back so they could see each other. Once he was sure Dustin would be still, he reached for an envelope he'd hidden and handed it to Dustin.

Dustin furrowed his eyebrows as he read the paperwork. He glanced at it for a minute then back at Shane. "Is this what I think it is?"

"Yup, from the tests we had done a few weeks back. I had 'em sent here since we don't have a permanent address."

"So we both came back clean? No more condoms?"

"If that's still what you want—for us to be exclusive."

"Hell yeah! Why wouldn't I wanna be just with you? I told you so many times that you're the hottest guy I know."

Shane rolled his eyes. "Then, yes, no more condoms."

Dustin gave Shane a solemn expression.

"What?" Shane asked.

"I've never done it without a condom. This'll be cool. But won't it be…different?" Dustin asked.

"We don't have to go without if you don't want to. Some couples always use condoms, for the mess."

"Yeah, messes don't bother me."

Dustin stood up in the Jeep and yanked down his jeans, his open shirt still flapping in the breeze. "Come on. I want that sucker inside me."

Shane drew his boyfriend to him. "I don't think we can manage anything in the Jeep. Let's at least get out of this cracker box."

He climbed out while Dustin struggled with his jeans. With a laugh, Shane reached up, grabbed Dustin around the waist and lifted him out.

Without pausing, Dustin shoved his pants down around his ankles and leaned across the hood. He glanced over his shoulder, almost panting in anticipation. "Well?"

Shane licked his lips at the sight of Dustin's tight, round ass. *That's prime butt.* He opened the cooler and withdrew a small bottle. When he stepped behind Dustin, he ran his hand over Dustin's ass cheeks.

"Come on. This is killing me!"

"Okay. It's gonna be cold, though." Shane dribbled the chilled gel down Dustin's ass crack.

"Fuck!" Dustin pressed against the vehicle, his ass gyrating. He twisted his half-naked body in some wild dance only Dustin could do. Shane ran his hands over Dustin's lithe back. The heat poured into Shane and brought his desire to a new level. He unzipped his jeans and lowered them enough to tug out his throbbing cock and rub it against Dustin.

"Do it. Shove it in. Damn, I need it so bad."

Shane considered Dustin's pleas and lust won out. He squirted more lubricant onto his cock and pressed forward. He let his cock kiss Dustin's hole then spear him. He paused and ran his hands down Dustin's side. A slight tremor traveled through Dustin as Shane pressed deeper. Dustin laid his head on the hood, his mouth slack and his breathing shallow.

"You okay?"

Dustin glanced back. "More. Shit."

Shane sank the rest of his length inside until he ground against Dustin's ass. He paused, relishing the pleasure of being inside his lover for the first time without a condom. The heat and sensations were incredible. Shane struggled to control himself. The urge to pound Dustin's ass nearly overwhelmed him.

Dustin pushed back, grinding himself against Shane. Soft mewling sounds came from him as Shane slowed his assault. Dustin moaned and arched his back. "Come on. Fuck me!"

Shane rammed forward. The friction against his uncovered cock took him to a new level of passion. Shane thrust faster. The passion of their lovemaking sent pulses of ecstasy through him. He pinned Dustin against the Jeep and shoved him into the perfect position for screwing. The fog of sex filled Shane as he fucked Dustin roughly. His climax began and at the last second, he rammed forward, trapped him and pumped days of cum into him. The sensations and emotions blended into a heady combination that left him floating. Dustin squirming under him came into focus as he moved closer to his climax.

With a final thrust, Dustin's orgasm ignited and his body convulsed. As the first stream shot across the tire,

Shane wrapped his arms around the cowboy, grabbed his nipples and twisted them.

"Ah, fuck!" Dustin screamed.

He bucked against Shane. His body trembled as he coated the tire with cum. His body spasmed several times until, with a final sigh, he collapsed over the hood.

"Fuck." Dustin gasped for air. "That was amazing."

Shane nodded in agreement as his cock slipped out and white cream seeped down Dustin's thigh. After he gathered the trail on his middle finger, he pushed the semen deep inside Dustin.

"You've never been so slick and hot before."

Dustin sprawled across the hood and sighed. "I've never had your load up my ass before. It's cool, but weird."

Shane rubbed Dustin's back. "Let's get you cleaned up and we can eat."

"Sounds like a fucking great idea. I'm starved!"

* * * *

Their round of hot cowboy sex had left Dustin famished. They'd dived into the basket and had eaten almost everything Shane had packed. Dustin licked his fingers one at a time, watching Shane as he did. *I want more time with him. Today was the first time we've connected like that and I'm hard again.* He glanced at Shane and again marveled at how well he and the hot bullfighter meshed. Dustin took a drink of his beer, enjoying the chill of the condensation dripping onto his chest. He drained the last of the bottle and surveyed the blanket covered with empty food containers. The relaxed meal had set a wonderful mood. Dustin leaned over and kissed Shane on the neck.

"You're making me horny, you know that?" Dustin said.

Shane smirked as he bit into the last piece of fried chicken. "You keep saying that, but I don't get it."

Dustin took the chicken from Shane and tossed it behind them. "I wanna fuck you. I've never fucked anyone without a rubber on."

"I thought you liked to bottom with me. We haven't switched since that first morning," Shane replied.

"Yeah, I know. But, like, I've never… But if you don't want to…"

Shane drew Dustin in for a kiss. "If you'd like to top, that'd be fun. You caught me by surprise. That's all."

Dustin's mood swung again and he bounced with excitement. "I want to know what it's like. 'Cause being catcher was damn hot. I want to fuck you until you come then keep screwing you like a crazy man."

Shane ran his hands over his chest and rubbed his own nipples as he listened to Dustin. "You'd like that? Fucking my butt through your own cum?"

"Oh, fuck yeah, that sounds hot."

Shane tugged off his shirt and tossed it to one side. Next were his boots. Jeans and underwear soon followed, leaving him naked and hard as he lay back on the blanket.

Dustin drank in the beauty of Shane's body. A clear bead formed at the tip of Shane's cock then ooze down the side. His attraction to Shane was stronger than ever as pulses of heat ran through his system. Dustin knew what he wanted. He wanted to give Shane the same experience he'd had earlier. Shane needed to enjoy the same mind-altering orgasm. Dustin stood and stripped then moved between Shane's legs.

He grabbed the bottle of lube, pushed one of Shane's legs up and drizzled the thick liquid down his cleft. After he trailed his fingers between Shane's muscular cheeks, Dustin sank a finger deep inside. The tight heat wrapped around Dustin's digit as he raked over Shane's prostate.

"Oh hell. That's nice." Shane fluttered his eyes shut.

The wind carried the delicious scent of Shane into the air around Dustin before disappearing. He added more lube and a second finger as he worked to loosen Shane for the pounding he had in mind. Shane's squirming underneath him ramped up Dustin's lust as he slipped in three fingers.

Shane trembled and sucked air through his teeth as Dustin stretched his ass. Dustin's cock ached as he worked to prepare his lover. Finally ready to bury his uncovered cock inside Shane for the first time, Dustin popped his fingers out and moved into position.

He coated his dick with lube, lifted Shane's legs to his shoulders then pushed himself inside. Shane gasped and his body shook as Dustin went at his ass with powerful strokes. Shane whimpered as Dustin slid his cock in again and again.

"How's that?" Dustin asked.

"Shit! Good."

"Ready for some slamming bull rider sex?"

Shane licked his lips and leered at Dustin, hooking his feet together behind Dustin's ass in answer. Shane pushed with his heels, urging Dustin to thrust faster. Dustin obliged and soon, with a few more hard strokes, Shane was writhing under him. Dustin dug his toes into the grass, lifting himself higher, and he slammed into Shane. Sweat dripped from Dustin as a familiar tingle radiated from his groin.

He hammered Shane, losing his rhythm as his climax hit. With a final powerful thrust, Dustin buried himself deep inside Shane's body as the first powerful jet shot from his cock.

"Oh fuck! I love you!" Dustin yelled.

The orgasm rolled over him as his balls emptied a second time. His body rippled in ecstasy as semen filled Shane. When the final wave washed over Dustin, he collapsed. His body twitched as they cooled, the breeze a welcome accompaniment. He wiggled forward and kissed Shane, but Shane's face wasn't filled with the satisfied pleasure he'd expected.

"What's wrong?"

Shane took Dustin's face between his hands and pressed their lips together. "Not a thing. That was crazy good. You're right."

Pride flowed through Dustin at Shane's praise. "Good, but next time I bottom."

Shane grabbed him as he moved off. "No, just stay like this. I don't need to get off again, I'm good. But this, this is what I want."

Dustin nodded, still floating in his own bliss.

Chapter Fourteen

Dustin ran around the outside of their trailer whooping in excitement at the rankings after the previous weekend's rodeo. He leaped on Shane, wrapping his legs tight. "The earnings are posted. I made it! I'm going to Vegas, baby!"

Shane hugged him tight. "That's great. I'm so proud of you."

"We need to celebrate. Hell, we need a blow-out party."

Shane glanced around then kissed Dustin. "It'd be fun to have a party, but we need to be careful."

"Careful? Since when are we careful?" Dustin stared at Shane, frustrated at his timid approach.

Shane checked around them again, never meeting Dustin's eyes. "We might try some caution. That's all. We don't want to draw attention."

Dustin jumped away from Shane and yelled. "I'm going to ride the meanest bulls at the national finals rodeo! Woop! Woop!"

Shane tried to calm him, but Dustin danced away. "Shane Rees is the best-looking man on the damn planet!"

His face turned deep red as he grabbed at Dustin. "Dammit! Shhh."

"And…he's a damn good kisser!" Dustin jumped and ran away laughing. He spun and launched himself at Shane, wrapping his arms and legs around him again. He kissed Shane until his muscles relaxed. Dustin uncoiled and dropped to his feet.

"I've never had a boyfriend before, especially a stud like you. I don't plan on being quiet about it." Dustin held Shane's face between his hands and stared into his eyes. "It scares the shit outta both of us that those assholes almost killed you because you're gay, but I won't hide who I am and how I feel about you anymore. Fuck them. Fuck them all!"

Shane shook his head and tried to turn away, but Dustin held him tight. "No. No more. Do you understand?"

"Yeah, okay. I don't want anything to happen to either of us."

"It's gonna be fine." One of his idiotic smiles burst across his face. "Hey, we were celebrating a few minutes ago. We're both going to Vegas!"

"I'm the alternate."

"You're there. That's all that matters. Right?" Dustin trotted over to their cooler, stuck his hands in the ice-filled water and fished out two beers. He handed over a cold bottle, unscrewed the top on his and took a swallow before explaining it again. "They don't take as many bullfighters as riders, and they vote on bullfighters. You're the youngest one. It's cool that you're at the finals."

"Yes, you keep reminding me." Shane drank part of his beer while he stared into the growing dimness of the New Mexico mountains as the campground settled in for the night. Shane sat until Dustin became impatient.

"What's going on?"

"It's that thing for my brother. I'm happy for him and all, but I can't help but consider... Well, he will have a family, and I never will." Shane slammed his bottle down onto the tailgate, sending glass everywhere. Dustin stepped up, took the broken bottle from Shane's clenched fist and checked his hand for injury. After he removed the few small shards that remained, he met Shane's gaze.

"You can still have a family. You always could. I'm having one. It's on my list."

"That's bullshit. Gay guys don't have families. Everyone knows that."

Dustin scowled. *Since when did I become the reasonable one?* "Bullshit is right. Darrin and Mitch have a family. They had pictures of their sons and grandkids everywhere. I remember them talking about them, so you're being a dick."

Dustin crossed his arms and for once let the silence stretch out. After a few long minutes, Shane jumped off the tailgate and paced. Dustin listened to the thump of each boot as it hit the ground.

He finally started to speak but Shane cut him off. "It'll be fine. I gave Sam what he wanted. Everybody's happy, right?"

Dustin became solemn. "Someday you're gonna have kids of your own."

Shane slowed and came to a stop. "So it's on your list, huh?"

"Yup, right after I get a kickass house. But I'm okay with a chain-link fence. It would keep the cattle outta the yard better than some little white picket thing." He waited, seeing that Shane was listening now. "You did a great thing. And you're gonna be a dad. That's amazing."

Shane ran his fingers through his hair. "No. Sam will be a dad, not me. But I guess I plan to be the uncle that spoils the kid rotten."

"So…does that make me an uncle, too?"

"What?"

"Well, since we're together… Does that mean I'm an uncle, too?"

Shane walked in front of Dustin and drew him in tight, tucking Dustin's head under his chin. "Yes, it does."

* * * *

A few days passed and Dustin had been thinking about the discussion regarding family they'd had recently. It had left Dustin thinking more about the topic than was typical for him. He'd come to realize that Todd and his parents were the people he felt closest to. He'd decided he needed to be more of a positive support for them, so he had made sure that he could be there to cheer on Todd during his ride.

Dustin bounced up and down on the fence as he waited to watch his friend. The buildup of excitement before his first go-round at the National Finals had left Dustin a frazzled bundle of nerves. The one thing saving him from losing his mind had been that Shane and Todd had made it, too. It had been questionable whether or not Todd's doctor would release him in time. Todd had ended up ranked above Dustin, but the winnings from the runs were high enough that someone could go from fifteenth place to winning the whole thing.

It relieved Dustin that Shane had shaken the fear he'd been dealing with over the attack. His attitude during those weeks had been something Dustin had hoped they wouldn't have to deal with again.

His own ride earlier had been okay, but this was the National Finals. The other bull riders were top-notch. He could live with a score of eighty-six out of a hundred. Dustin wiped the sweat from his palms. Todd was up now. Shane watched from the other side of the arena and, even though he wasn't in the ring, Dustin was glad he was close in case something happened. Shane would save the day if things went wrong, even if Dustin understood deep down that sometimes things went to shit and no one could do anything about it.

Todd had drawn a bull named Dulce. It was one of the few bulls at the finals that Dustin hadn't ridden. All the bulls here were the best, so Dulce would give Todd a high-scoring ride. Dustin couldn't help but compare his bull to Todd's. His competitive nature pushed him to win, even against his best friend.

A loud bang drew his attention to the chute. Immediately, Dustin realized Todd was having trouble. Every time he lowered himself onto the bull's back, it would throw its head and try to pin Todd's leg against the gate. After a handful of false starts, Todd settled on. The waiting left Dustin's nerves shot. He locked his eyes on his friend as Todd's black cowboy hat flipped back and forth in a nod. *Thank God! I wondered if they'd ever start.*

The bull exploded from the chute, bucking as high as a bronc. Its back coiled down, then snapped back with enough force to make Dustin wince. The bull jerked into a spin, trying to rid itself of the troublesome cowboy. Dustin could almost feel Todd's legs clamp around the big animal. The bull whipped out of its spin and started a bucking run across the arena.

The clock ticked down and Dustin muttered, "Come on, Todd. Just a few more seconds. Come on!"

The animal managed an impossible maneuver, switched nose for tail and Todd slid.

"Damn it! Hang on!"

Todd slipped again and Dustin groaned when Todd lost his grip. A gasp from the crowd snapped Dustin's focus back. Todd had tangled in his bull rope and was being dragged across the hard-packed dirt. The two bullfighters rushed in to help, but they couldn't untangle Todd from the rosin-coated rope.

Dustin glanced across the arena to see Shane pressed against the fence, his face pinched and his focus on Todd. It felt as if hours crawled past as the efforts of the bullfighters focused on getting Todd out uninjured. With a sudden lurch, Todd's hand broke free and he landed in a sprawling pile in the middle of the arena.

Without pausing, the bull flipped ends, lowered its head and charged the unseated cowboy. Todd staggered to his feet before the bull hit him like a semi. It horrified Dustin when Todd folded in half over the ton of beef hitting him in the back. Judging by Todd's scream, the injury was bad. One bullfighter ran from the side to distract the animal. His effort earned him a sideswipe of Dulce's horns that left the bullfighter crumpled on the arena floor.

Dustin climbed the fence with some half-baked idea of rescue. The bull dropped its head and charged again. It ground Todd into the arena dust. The bull backed off for a second. Todd lay like a broken GI Joe doll. A strangled gasp escaped Dustin's lips. The horsemen separated the bull from the broken bodies. A fog of disbelief engulfed Dustin as the EMTs carried Todd from the arena.

A hand landed on Dustin's shoulder. He ripped around, ready to dismember whoever had broken his focus. He threw a violent punch, trying to pull it when he realized it was Shane, but he still delivered a good pop.

"Damn. Glad to see you, too." Shane rubbed his hand over his jaw. "Take a breath. The ambulance left with Todd already. They'll be at the ER in a few minutes. I know you want to be there, but you can't help him right now. I'll take you over as soon as the last ride ends. I have to fill in for Pete. The horn he took to the chest tore him up."

Dustin froze in place, still stunned. "Okay, thanks. I just need to be there for Todd. He's… His family is…" He shrugged, unable to put his emotions into words.

Shane nodded and rubbed his hand over the back of Dustin's neck. "It won't be long. I've already talked to the other bullfighters and they know I'm going to the hospital as soon as we're done. I swear. I'll be as quick as I can."

"I know. I know there's nothing I can do, but I need to be there."

Shane patted Dustin's back again. He leaned into the touch, needing Shane's support as fear filled him. Shane tightened his hand with a comforting strength.

"Come on. You can fill me in while I get dressed after this last ride."

Dustin wondered what was going on. "Aren't you afraid everyone will find out about us?"

"We need each other." Shane said. "I've been considering what you said and you're right. We can't live our lives hiding. It's time they get over some of their shit. And if they can't, they can fucking stay outta my business."

"Okay, sounds good."

* * * *

Dustin raced into the hospital, afraid of what he'd find. Shane had brought him over as soon as the event had ended, but the entire Martin family was in the waiting room while Todd was undergoing a complicated surgery to put the pieces back together. They had all been so focused on Todd that no one had questioned Shane's presence during the resulting hours. When the surgery was over and Todd had been assigned a room, he and Shane waited until some of the family had left before trying to see him. Dustin eased around the corner to find Todd's mother sitting in the chair beside the bed. She glanced up and relief flooded Dustin at her smile.

"Come on in, Dustin. Todd's still groggy from the anesthesia. But they say in six months or so, he'll be able to ride again."

"If my mommy lets me," came the faint grumble from the bed.

"Todd! Damn, you scared me!" Dustin said.

"Shh, this is a hospital, asshole. You can't go around yelling."

"Todd! Your language," said his mom.

"Yes, ma'am."

Todd not spewing obscenities was so foreign to Dustin that he couldn't help but laugh. It showed him that Todd would be okay. Todd's eyes drifted shut and fluttered open to focus on Dustin. "Where's the squeeze? He brought you, right?"

Dustin's gaze darted between the two Martins, not sure what to say or do, afraid that Todd's mother might not be as accepting as Todd had claimed.

Todd let out a groan as he moved to a more comfortable position. He rolled his eyes at Dustin. "Oh holy—" Todd glanced at his mother. "Shoot. You left Shane waiting, didn't you? Go get him, dumb…head."

Dustin glanced at Todd's mother. She nodded in agreement. He went to the door and motioned for Shane to come into the room. They walked back in together. Todd's mother was helping him get a sip of water. He swallowed and relaxed against the pillow. Once he settled again, he smirked at the pair.

"Hey, Shane. How are you doing these days?"

"I didn't lose an argument with an angry bull, so I'm doing pretty well. I've healed up fine, just like you will."

Todd's eyes sagged shut, then popped open as he fought off sleep. "Wish you'd have been in there. Maybe you'd have got me loose before that bad boy tried to grind me into the dirt."

Shane shook his head. "Those guys are good. I couldn't have done any better."

"Yeah? None of them jumped the bull to help me."

"I haven't done that again, either."

There was silence then soft breathing as Todd succumbed to the medication. Dustin glanced around, not sure what to do.

"Dustin, are you going to introduce me to your friend?" Mrs. Martin asked.

Panic washed over him. "Um, sure. No problem, Mrs. M. Yeah, like, ahuh. This is Shane." He paused and swallowed hard, not sure he was ready for this, but said it anyway. "He's my boyfriend."

She stood and leaned over Todd's sleeping form to shake Shane's hand. "Good to meet you. Please call me Kris. I wish Dustin had seen fit to fill me in sooner. Todd's told me a bit about you, though. Dustin must wonder if I'm going to go all fundamentalist on his ass because he's gay. He doesn't get that I've known ever since he and Todd became friends."

Dustin's mouth hung open.

"What? I can't say ass?" Kris asked.

Dustin's mouth stayed open as the surprise worked through his system. He swallowed, closed his mouth and changed subjects.

"How is he?" Dustin motioned toward Todd.

Kris' lips flattened as she considered her son. "The bull broke his left leg. They've put pins and plates in it. They said they treated the injury the same as they would any other professional athlete so he can go back to bull riding."

Dustin nodded, filling in the gaps. "Bull riding is all he knows, though."

"No. He *thinks* rodeo is all he knows. He's like my other stubborn bull-riding son who doesn't see he has talents beyond the arena."

Dustin was stunned as he processed her words. He worked his mouth several times like a fish that had been out of water too long.

"You better close that thing before you draw flies," Kris said.

Shane's snorted response destroyed any remaining strands of seriousness.

Dustin turned to his sleeping friend, put his hand on his shoulder and reached up to wipe a tear from his eye.

* * * *

Shane's gut twisted into a knot from the first jump of Dustin's ride the next day. The series of crow hops across the arena had Dustin bouncing on the bull's back. Shane hovered a few yards away, ready to step in at the first sign of trouble. At the sound of the buzzer, his tension left. Dustin dismounted in a heap. His clenched jaw was obvious as he left the arena. The few riders left passed quickly, but Shane didn't miss Dustin watching through the fence and seething.

The short ride to their hotel room went by in tense silence and Dustin never glanced in Shane's direction as he stomped down the hallway to their room. Shane followed him through the door, growing annoyed with the childish show Dustin was staging. He waited while Dustin took off the first spur and was working on the other, his anger only seeming to build.

"You want to talk about why you're all pissy?"

Shane dodged the metal spurs that crashed into the wall behind him. He glanced at the small pile of steel and leather at the base of the hotel wall and back at Dustin.

"Did that make you feel better?" he asked.

"Don't fucking patronal me," was Dustin's curt reply.
"Patronize — and I wasn't."

Dustin's face turned scarlet as his hands squeezed into fists. "Shut your fucking mouth, you asshole."

Shane crossed his arms. "You want to be mad? Fine. But there's no reason for you to be pissed with me."

Dustin made another circuit of the room and pounced. "You fucked it up! You were too close and spooked the bull!"

"That's not true. We stay close to the fence unless something happens. There's not anything I can do if your bull does nothing but run and crow hop. Why didn't you spur him? What were you waiting on?"

Dustin's voice verged on hysterical. "Fuck you, asshole! I spurred the bastard through the whole thing. I worked my ass off, not just standing in the damn arena flapping my arms like a big, fucking penguin."

Shane stiffened. "I was doing my job, something you apparently don't understand. I rescued pretty-boy bull riders like you all day long."

Dustin spun toward Shane. "You think I don't work? That I'm lazy? Fuck you! You don't do shit all day but prance around the arena." Dustin sucked in air, obviously far past being reasonable. "And I'm tired of you and the pity party over that damn scar."

Shane's anger flared to incendiary. "You self-centered little shit. Don't you dare tell me how I feel."

Shane's head snapped back when Dustin punched him. He wiped the trickle of blood from his mouth as he glared at Dustin. "Did that make you a man? Do you feel better now? Go ahead. Hit me again if that's what it takes for you to grow a pair of balls." Shane tilted his chin toward Dustin.

"Fuck you! You don't get to be all goody two-shoes. You and your fucking scar can go to hell!"

Shane's body knotted in anguish, tears searing the corners of his eyes. It was like being kicked in the gut again. *There! I knew it. The whole 'it's sexy' shit was fake. This is exactly what I thought would happen. He's just like everyone else.* Blood dribbled down Shane's face as he stared at Dustin in disbelief. *How can he do this after all we've been through? Winning finals ranks more important than what we are, I guess. I will not be second choice for anyone.* He wiped off the blood with his sleeve while he locked his eyes on Dustin. Without a word, Shane grabbed his bag and threw it over his shoulder.

"Where are you going? Can't finish a fight? Going to run off to lick your wounds?"

"Find someone else to play mind games with. I'm done." Shane walked out of the door, letting it close behind him.

* * * *

Shane had begun questioning what he had said from the instant the door had slammed shut behind him. The time since then had been a blur. Shane couldn't recall any details from the incident. By the time he reached the dressing room at the next day's events to prepare for his time in the ring, he was a tangled mass of emotions. He struggled to work out what had happened with Dustin. There were only a few more rounds in the finals and things were going well. Dustin had placed again tonight, but they hadn't talked since Shane had walked out.

"Hey, big brother, how's life?"

Shane turned to see Sam walking toward him. He tried to plan a response, but his mind was so tied up in his problems with Dustin that he couldn't think of anything else. He shrugged and went back to applying his makeup. "A few minutes isn't much older, little brother."

"No, maybe not."

Shane worked for a short time before Sam held a hand out for the makeup. "You should be better at this by now, but I can help with your makeup. Your hands don't seem steady today."

Shane handed over the brush and soon Sam was filling in the ovals around his eyes. After a few minutes, Shane chuckled in spite of his dark mood. Sam paused and lifted his eyebrows. "Yes?"

"You still stick your tongue out of the side of your mouth when you concentrate."

Sam stuck his thumb into the middle of Shane's forehead and pushed until his head tilted backward. The brush glided over his skin. Sam's face was a study in concentration. Shane opened his mouth to dispel the gathering silence.

Sam stopped him. "Shut up. If you talk, it'll crack the paint. Give it a chance to dry. Besides, from what I hear, you and Dustin did plenty of talking the other night."

Shane widened his eyes and Sam shrugged then continued. "You're surprised that I know? Really? You thought the two of you could have a screaming, knock-down, drag-out fight and no one would hear you? And you know the rodeo people are some of the worst gossips. My friends made sure I knew."

Shane lifted his head as Sam changed the color he was using before he continued painting his face. "You also should know you're going to be an uncle. A dad. Oh hell, you know what I mean."

Shane held his mouth tight and muttered, "I'm the uncle. *You're* the dad."

Sam finished with the red and put in the last details. "Yeah, since I'll be the one doing the late-night shitty-diaper patrol, I'm the dad." He focused to add the last outline strokes before stopping. Straightening, he caught Shane's gaze.

"Don't tell anyone. No one else knows. Angie doesn't want anyone to, in case something happens, goes wrong."

Shane beamed at Sam and grabbed his shoulder. "It'll be fine. I'm excited for you two."

Sam put away the paints and brushes while Shane checked his work in the mirror. "Nice job, Sam. You could stick around and do my makeup every night."

A snort erupted from his brother. "Yeah, I don't think so. Some of us have real jobs. I drove out to see how you were doing."

Shane punched his arm playfully. "Sucks to be you. I'd rather run at pissed-off bulls."

"Yeah, haven't you broken about everything? And..." Sam cast an expression of displeasure at the scar traveling down his sibling's face.

Shane scowled at his brother. "Don't tell me you're starting that shit, too?"

Sam started to respond then sat beside Shane. "You know you have to talk to him. Sounds like both of you said things you shouldn't have. But that shit happens. No marriage is perfect." Sam waved his hand when Shane started to correct him. "No, you aren't married, but you're living together and probably feeling like you are. But being with someone isn't all blossoms and bullshit. Sometimes you gotta be the one to say sorry, even if you don't think it's your fault."

"He said things that are gonna be hard to forgive."

"Yeah, when you're that close to someone, they know all your buttons."

"Part of me doesn't want to forgive him. That was a damn low blow."

"So you can't forgive Dustin for being angry and stupid? Because if you can't, you're going to have a long, lonely life."

Shane glared at him before letting out a heavy sigh. "Well, that's fucked up."

"Welcome to the world of relationships. Now get dressed and go talk to Dustin before something happens and it gets worse."

Shane rolled his eyes. "Dammit! I hate it when you're right."

* * * *

Dustin glared at Todd from his seat beside the hospital bed.

"What do you mean, 'stop fucking around?'. I'm here because you almost died and I told your mom I'd keep an eye on you while she got some sleep."

"Bullshit. You've screwed up with Shane and you're panicking, so you've been sitting in here with me to keep from dealing with the mess you made. Just admit it. You love Shane and you got all pissy because you didn't make the rankings one night and you crapped all over him. Man up! Go talk to your boyfriend." Todd let out a snicker. "I'm sure he'd like to see you grabbing your balls, anyway."

Dustin searched for something to throw at his best friend but found nothing but Todd's half-filled urine bottle, which derailed Dustin's line of thought. "You know, that's just nasty. Nasty old piss in a bottle sitting there. Probably leave it there when you eat, too."

"Damn, you're easy to mess with. You always have been. I bet you forgot your meds again today, didn't you?"

"Oh, shut up, I remembered my meds." Dustin glanced around, trying to remember. "I'm pretty sure, anyway."

"Oh God." Todd shook his head. "Get out of here. I'll take another happy pill and sleep. Because I'll be at the last round and you're going to win this thing. Now go find Shane and beg him to take you back." Todd waved Dustin toward the door. "Offer him sex, because you're worthless for anything else."

"Oh, screw you, Martin! I can work circles around you any day." It was impossible to stay moody around Todd. "Your mom says that barrel racer keeps coming to see you."

Todd waved his hand at Dustin, not meeting his gaze as his cheeks turned scarlet. "Her? I barely know her. Can't even remember her name."

"Uh-huh, sure."

Todd nodded as the nurse came in with his meds. He upended the cup and washed them down with a few drinks of water. He nodded at Dustin again. "Go. Please. Talk to Shane before tonight's round. Then win this year's National Finals."

Dustin patted Todd's shoulder. "Okay, okay. Quit bitching at me."

Todd's mother walked in as they finished. From her expression, it was obvious she'd heard their conversation. She gave Dustin a slight smile. "I'm here for Todd. Go talk to Shane."

He started to argue, but when she cocked an eyebrow, he remained silent. With a snort from Todd, he gave her a hug and slipped out of the door to find Shane. Once he arrived at the arena, he had searched everywhere he thought was a possibility. Close to taking desperate measures, he was making a last search through the area when he glanced up to see Shane stretching on the opposite side. Dustin raced toward him. He skidded to a stop and grabbed Shane's arm.

"Hey, I gotta—"

"Damn! Dustin. I've been—"

"No, man. Listen. I was—"

"It's okay. I know—"

"No, no. Listen I was a dumbsh—"

Shane held up his hands as the words tumbled from both of them. "Okay, hang on. One at a time."

Dustin broke in. "Yeah. Okay. Well, I was an idiot. I don't know why I said what I did. I don't want anything to come between us. I don't want us to break up because I'm in a bad mood that has nothing to do with the two of us."

Shane sighed. "Yeah, well, I should have been more understanding and not so temperamental. That's me being a super-sensitive asshole."

Dustin let out a breath and wrapped his arms around Shane. "I've been stewing about this since it happened. Well, since you walked out and I realized I'd messed up."

"Yeah, I've been considering everything about it, too. Sam chewed my ass and told me to come talk to you."

Dustin nodded. "Todd bitched me out, as well. He said to come back and beg you to forgive me." He cut his eyes to the floor. "Todd was right."

Shane kissed Dustin. "We're going to have fights, but we need to get better at them not tearing us apart."

Dustin hung on to Shane for another moment then released him. With a grin plastered over his face, he whispered, "I hear makeup sex is outstanding. I have a few days of cum stored up."

Shane laughed at Dustin's antics, relieved they'd gotten a lesson in keeping their relationship working with no long-term damage. There would be more problems, but it was a good step in learning what not to do and how to manage it better the next time. "Win tonight and we'll do whatever you want."

"That's a promise that I'll hold you to."

He glanced at Dustin. "Hey, which bull did you draw for the final go-round?"

Dustin grimaced. "Diablo."

Chapter Fifteen

Dustin glanced out into the arena, relieved when he saw Shane. *Glad things got ironed out between us.* His focus narrowed until it was just him and the bull. He created a small, quiet space in his mind. As he watched for the perfect opening, the lunges of the massive animal under him seemed to slow. Dustin dropped with catlike sureness and cinched his legs around his adversary. Only marginally aware of the activities going on around him, he played out the various scenarios once the gate opened. The elements came together. He gave a quick nod and it swung open in a slow arc. In agonizing detail, Dustin sensed the corded muscles under him contract then uncoil. The bull left a trail of glistening froth as it moved to rid itself of the annoyance of having Dustin on its back.

Dustin swept forward with the first jump. His muscles knotted as he rode the center of a crescent of primitive strength. The bull's second jump threw Dustin backward as the twin hooves swept out and the muscles exploded with effort. Dustin countered each of the moves in a savage dance set to an eight-second finale. The magnified sense of being continued, allowing Dustin to expect each movement of the bull before it happened. The world slowed to a crawl as the intricacies of the battle between him and Diablo played out.

Diablo tensed under Dustin. He was going to sunfish. The roll began and Dustin sensed that instant of suspension before the ton of beef under him snapped outward in a violent explosion of power. The maneuver had unseated Dustin the last time he'd been on this bull. This time, Dustin's focus was needle-sharp, and he flowed in perfect unison.

Dustin glimpsed Shane following his every move. The sight of Shane's worried face and the thought of his love for Shane broke his focus. Suddenly, the howl of the crowd, the sharp bite of the dust-filled air, the speed and ferocity of the animal... Everything crashed into his conscious thought.

The ride continued as Dustin flowed with each movement of the bull in perfect timing and balance. The flying belly roll Diablo loved to use was a bust. Dustin snapped his head around. His helmet and face-guard whistled through the still air. Then the instant he'd been dreading happened. He moved a millisecond out of time with the bull. *The easy part is over. Now comes the real work.*

Diablo's head almost grazed the arena floor before shooting upward. Dustin's body took a beating and he slipped. His heels locked in the bull's flanks as he fought to stay on. But he fought for firm seating with too many seconds left.

Dustin had gotten a few magic seconds where the path from one jump to the next was clear. Now he had only a few seconds to go on a bull determined to fuck him up and make him a loser.

Dustin's arm cramped. His biceps fought each buck as the effects of the previous nine rides showed. He held his legs like bands of iron around the bull, battling each jump and twist. The sinew of his body strained under the beating Diablo delivered with the professional detachment of a Mafia hit man.

The animal's muscles tightening signaled the change into another spin. This time, Dustin's boot heel slipped and his weight shifted. He clamped his thighs as tightly as possible, trying to eke out the final milliseconds. He began to lose his seating, struggled to power back onto this monster then felt himself heading for the arena dirt.

For a split second, overwhelming disappointment hit. *I'm losing. Again. Am I destined to always lose?* He glanced about in desperation. *Shane.* The unmistakable admiration showing on his lover's face filled Dustin. *I may not win, but I won't quit.*

Dustin locked his body, digging his foot into the bull's thick hide. His thighs burned with exertion when he caught a break. Diablo paused for a heartbeat and Dustin lurched back into his seat. A smile crept across his face as the eight-second buzzer sounded and the crowd thundered with applause.

Triumph flooded him. As his grip loosened on the rope, he used the animal's next jump to launch himself. His arc carried him through the air to land on his feet, pumping his arms at the raucous crowd.

The crowd clapped wildly, showing their approval of Dustin's bravado-filled dismount and he basked in the glory of his ride. But a motion drew his eye to the side. Diablo had decided Dustin didn't need adoration. The bull had something else in mind for him.

Shane screamed, "Incoming!" and launched toward them.

Damn! That bull is out for my blood.

The bull paused, his brindled hide twitching as he swung his blunt horns from side to side. His snort sounded across the arena as he considered Dustin then launched a jet of dust into the air with his hoof.

Dustin's stomach knotted at the sight of the massive animal speeding toward him. A second later the fence became the goal for one enraged bull, two bullfighters and him. *All of us are racing for our lives.*

Dustin knew he couldn't reach the fence in time. *Dammit! This bull will not get me.* Shane launched himself in a repeat of his maneuver from months before. But as Shane shot over Diablo, the bull swung his head. His forearm-thick horn connected with Shane's jaw and Dustin's boyfriend fell like a sack of feed.

With Shane out cold, the focus of the arena was on Dustin. He raced toward Shane as the horsemen managed to get the bull into the holding corral. Fortunately, fucking up a cowboy didn't seem to be his destiny today.

The instant the bull was safely behind metal fences and gates, the arena filled with people who were there to help. Within a few seconds, Shane was strapped to the stretcher and they were sprinting to the dressing room where they laid him onto the table. Dustin's panic was barely controlled as the love of his life became buried under a cadre of medical professionals.

Through the entire event, Dustin kept up a steady chant. "OhmyGod, ohmyGod, ohmyGod. Shane, wake up. Wake up. Please."

Shane cracked open his eyes and ran his tongue over dry lips. "Dustin, hush," he said.

His brief statement caused everyone to renew their efforts working on Shane. A medic forced Dustin away while the others pushed, prodded and shone lights into every opening in Shane's head. But after a litany of questions, she rocked back and patted Shane's forearm.

"Seems like you'll be fine, but since you were out so long, I'd recommend an X-ray."

Shane sat up, turning and twisting to check every muscle. He seemed to have arrived at the same conclusion. "Everything's okay. I have to go back."

The medic shook her head. "I can't stop you. You damn rodeo idiots."

Shane signed the waiver paperwork stuck in front of him as Dustin stayed at his side. He handed everything back to the EMT and studied Dustin. "There're only a couple more riders. I'm not hurt, just a headache. I'll be fine."

"You sure? I heard what she said. Don't be stupid. It scared the shit out of me when you didn't wake up."

"Come on. Help me up. You can stand on the sidelines and worry about me for a change." He leaned closer to whisper to Dustin, "I think you earned that reward we talked about, too."

Confused for a few seconds, Dustin beamed at Shane. "Yeah, and you make damn sure I get it."

* * * *

Shane lay in the hot tub with Dustin against his chest. The hot swirling water worked miracles on his sore muscles. After the finals had ended, Dustin had splurged and moved them to a room with a Jacuzzi.

They both were taking full advantage of all the perks of the high-end hotel.

"I could get used to this."

"Hmm." Dustin turned and touched his lips to Shane's. "Yeah, I could, too. Makes me feel lazy."

Shane caressed Dustin's torso. The heat of his desire for Dustin was far greater than the heat of the water. He hesitated, not wanting another argument, especially when their relationship was on the mend. But he decided it was like getting out a sandburr — the quicker the better.

Their eyes met. "Are you pissed off about not winning it all?" Shane asked.

Dustin clearly first considered the question then shrugged. "Well, I'm not thrilled. I wanted to win, and I did ride that damn Diablo. But a bunch of people want to sponsor me now, so no more living out of your tiny little trailer. I'll try again next year. They're all amazed I got this far when I'm only twenty-one." Dustin studied Shane. "Are you disappointed? Your bad-ass bull-rider boyfriend didn't win."

"You placed in the top few riders almost every round, won a couple and came out with the second-highest earnings your first time at the finals. I'm proud as hell of you!"

Dustin beamed and leaned against Shane's chest, pressing their lips together. "Good. I'd never want to disappoint you."

Shane wrapped his hand around the back of Dustin's neck and drew them together for a heated kiss. They separated with a soft pop. "Never gonna happen."

They floated in the hot water, touching as the warmth soaked away their aches. Shane sat up and ran his hand over Dustin's body. As he studied his boyfriend's sparkling blue eyes, he thought about how lucky he was to have found the love of his life. *I'm sure I haven't finished dealing with all my crap. With Dustin here, everything will be fine. He seems to always be able to snap me out of my moodiness.* He kissed the edge of Dustin's ear then whispered, "I ordered us some snacks while you showered. Let's see if they got it right."

Dustin nodded, climbed out of the tub and grabbed a towel to dry himself. Shane followed, enjoying the sight of Dustin's cloth-wrapped body within touching distance. Crystalline drops studded Dustin's shoulders before Shane dried him off. Dustin sighed when Shane ran the towel over his butt. He spread his legs and grabbed the side of the tub when Shane ran the cloth along the inside of his boyfriend's thighs. Shane rubbed the cloth against Dustin's heat-stretched sac, drying the sensitive skin.

Dustin's erection jutted before him when he took the towel from Shane. "My turn. Spin around."

Shane winked, eager for Dustin's touch. The soft towel skated over his shoulders as Dustin wiped off the moisture. He swiped between Shane's ass cheeks. Dustin slid his hands around Shane's waist and cupped his package.

"Food. Food first," Shane said.

"All I need is your sausage," Dustin teased.

"Yeah, but not very filling— Well, you can't actually eat— Oh, shut up!"

Dustin walked toward the room-service cart. As he moved past, Shane yanked the cloth from Dustin's trim waist. "Oh no, mister. You're the one who likes to be naked all the time."

Soft laughter drifted back as Dustin shook his ass. "Works for me. Come on. I'm hungry. What did you get us?"

"Lift off the big cover."

Dustin raised his eyebrows then uncovered the largest dish.

"Fuck yes! Strawberries and chocolate. I love strawberries and chocolate." He wrapped Shane in a tight hug. "You remembered!"

Shane gave him a gentle kiss. "Try it. The guy said they were 'fabulous'."

Dustin grabbed one of the golf-ball-size strawberries by its long stem, ran it through the chocolate sauce, lifted it to his mouth and bit into the flesh of the ripe berry. He chewed, darting his tongue out to catch a drop on his lip. A second bite finished off the massive fruit, and Dustin licked his fingers clean. His face radiated happiness. "Oh hell, that's good. Here. Try one!"

Dustin dredged another berry across the thick sauce and lifted it to Shane's lips. The aroma of chocolate mixed with Dustin's fresh, clean musk sent tingles into Shane's system. He pierced the ripe berry and sweet flavors flooded his mouth. The rich chocolate mixed with the fruit and swept through Shane's senses. As the flavors subsided, he realized Dustin's palm had a pool of chocolate in its center.

Cupping Dustin's hand in his, Shane ran his tongue over his palm for a taste of the sweet sauce. He focused on the Dustin-infused bits of chocolate until a low mewing came from his boyfriend. Dustin panted, his cock leaking pre-cum. Shane ran his finger through the sauce and smeared it over Dustin's hard nipple. He dove in to lick the small, erect point.

"Ah, man! That's good."

Shane smeared Dustin's other nipple with sauce then cleaned it with his tongue and lips. Dustin shook with each pass. His moans of appreciation increased in volume. Shane threw Dustin across his shoulder and carried him to bed. He slapped his bare ass then tossed him to the mattress. Dustin pushed himself up to stare at Shane.

"So, you're in charge tonight. What'd you have planned?" Shane asked.

Dustin leered. "More chocolate licking."

Shane grabbed the container of chocolate and crawled between Dustin's legs. Never taking his eyes from Dustin, he again trailed a finger through the rich sauce. Once it was covered in dark deliciousness, he spread a line on the underside of Dustin's rock-hard cock. He danced his tongue along its length until Dustin arched his body in pleasure. He smeared more chocolate around the deep red crown then Shane slipped it into his mouth like a lollipop. When he dragged his tongue over the slit, Dustin restrained him.

"Stop! I'm gonna shoot, and I don't want to yet."

Shane ran his fingers over Dustin's balls then tugged on them. "What do you want, then?"

Dustin lifted himself to his elbows. "My turn." He took the chocolate from Shane and crawled until their crotches pressed against each other, their wet, hard lengths sliding together. His eyelids fluttered shut as Shane reveled in the ecstatic feelings that washed over him.

The scent of chocolate flooded his senses. He snapped his eyes open as Dustin traced his sauce-covered finger over Shane's lips, where he then kissed and worked his tongue until he'd recovered every drop. Then, to

Shane's shock, Dustin traced his chocolate-coated finger down the scar on his face. He started to protest then realized the sensations Dustin brought out were anything but unpleasant. With each swipe of Dustin's tongue, Shane's feelings about the scar twisted and transformed. His mind came to understand that the mark was just a part of him, not the thing that defined his life—the exact thing Dustin had been trying to tell him since they'd met.

When Dustin loaded another finger, Shane intercepted it and guided the coated digit to his mouth. He nursed the chocolate off, then licked and nipped at it like a small cock. Dustin ran his finger over Shane's teeth then leaned in and kissed him, grabbing his lip between his teeth before releasing it and sitting back with a smile.

"Ever fucked anyone wearing chaps?" Dustin asked.

Shane propped himself on his elbows. "Seriously? You wanna try it?"

Dustin ground against Shane's cock with small circles of his ass. "Yeah. It sounds mind blowing." Dustin paused then asked, "Is that okay?"

"The best-looking dude I've ever seen wants me to fuck him with his riding chaps on and wants to know if it's okay? Oh, hell yes!"

Dustin jumped from the bed to the small pile of clothes where they lay. He buckled on the custom-made leather. Shane ran his tongue over his lips at the sight of Dustin's pale skin highlighted against the chaps. Dustin moved his round butt past Shane and the scent of leather wafted over him, combining with Dustin's spicy scent into a powerful aphrodisiac. The sight of Dustin's hard cock jutting from the hand-tooled leather made Shane's dick flex and a knot form in his stomach.

Dustin tugged at the fringe on his chaps. Every nerve in Shane's body lit on fire for the man standing in front of him. "Holy shit. You're fucking sexy!"

Dustin reached down and stroked his cock. "Oh yeah? You think you'd like to tap this?"

"Damn, babe. You have me ready to come just from watching you." Shane picked up the bottle of lube, but Dustin had a peculiar expression on his face.

"What?" Shane asked.

"Well…"

Shane realized Dustin wanted to try something new. "Spit it out. I bet I'll like it."

"I thought…maybe…you'd like to watch?" Dustin made a vague motion at the lube.

Shane shuffled through the words, taking time to understand the offer. He smiled with what probably looked more like a leer and he tossed the bottle to Dustin. "Fuck yeah! I'd *love* to watch."

Dustin grinned from ear to ear and skittered across the bed. He leaned against the headboard and spread his legs. Shane lay across the foot of the bed, teasing his cock and balls, ready to enjoy the show. Dustin popped open the lube and squeezed a blob onto the tips of his fingers. He lowered them between his legs and smeared the gel up and down his crack. After coating the cleft of his ass, he eased his middle finger inside.

"Oh fuck. That's nice. What do you think?" Dustin asked.

Shane rubbed pre-cum over the head of his cock, forcing himself to stop before he lost it. "Oh God, Dustin. You're so hot."

Dustin added another finger with a gasp. "Oh, man, a little burn now. But I need to get ready for that curved monster of yours."

Shane kissed the inside of Dustin's knee. "You're so fuckable. Don't get too carried away, though."

"A little less porn talk, huh?"

"Just a touch."

Dustin closed his eyes as he squirmed around his fingers.

Shane moved closer, the wet sound of Dustin fingering himself a siren's call. The scent of earth, musk and sex whirled in an intoxicating blend. Dustin slid his fingers out. He added more lube to his hand and plunged three fingers into his ass. Shane ran his hands over Dustin's leather-covered legs, moistening his lips as he stared.

Dustin furrowed his brow as he froze in place. "I'm kinda tight. It's been a few days."

Shane stroked Dustin's leg, toying with the thick fringe of the chaps. "Take your time. We've got all night."

"I don't! I plan to get fucked soon."

Shane cut his answering chuckle short when Dustin's head dropped back and he pressed his fingers hard into himself. His breath was shallow and rapid from the effort. Shane reached the edge of orgasm repeatedly and was approaching it again when Dustin moaned out, "Fuck me! Ah, shit. Now, I'm ready."

Shane scrambled to comply, grabbing the backs of Dustin's thighs, lifting them and exposing his entrance. The smell of leather and sex bombarded him and shoved him to the edge again. He slid his hands over the chaps as he folded Dustin in half.

Dustin locked eyes with him and Shane recognized that Dustin shared a similar hunger. He gasped as Shane pressed the head of his aching cock against Dustin's slick hole. Dustin glared at him. "Fuck me! Goddammit! Fuck me! Shove it in!"

Dustin's cries drove Shane forward. He flexed his ass, pressing himself slowly into Dustin in spite of his cries for more. Soon his crotch ground against Dustin's ass. Dustin arched his body as he twisted his own nipples. "Shit. So good."

Shane rubbed against him, the tight heat sending waves of pleasure through his body. His cock throbbed as he fought to hold out. Dustin squirmed toward him, clearly wanting more. Unable to wait, Shane grabbed the leather chaps and slammed repeatedly into Dustin.

"Shit! Oh fuck!" Dustin groaned.

Shane tried to hit Dustin's prostate each time he slid inside. Reduced to inarticulate cries, Dustin writhed as Shane pounded him. Every muscle in Shane's body drove forward with each thrust. Dustin's ass constricted around Shane's cock and a guttural moan soon vibrated the walls.

"Shit! Coming!"

Dustin ground against Shane, his body shaking. He shot, covering them with cum. Dustin shook as he exploded onto them. The last shot oozed onto Dustin's stomach and he sagged against the bed.

Shane pounded harder, racing toward his climax. Just when Shane thought his euphoria had peaked, a new level of intense pleasure coursed through his nipples. He opened his eyes to see Dustin attached to the nubs with his fingers like a pair of jumper cables, and the electricity flowing through them would have started a truck. Shane pinned Dustin under him and emptied his balls. Shane's cum filled Dustin's ass as the wet sounds of amazing sex echoed in the room. He shivered as the final wave rolled over him.

"God, I love how you work my butt."

"I love you, Dustin."

Both men froze. Shock coursed through Shane, but he realized his statement was true. *I do love Dustin.*

Dustin's expression was pure joy. "Took you long enough. And I'm supposed to be the one who can't focus."

Dustin locked his heels behind Shane's thighs. "Don't pull out. I want you in me forever."

Shane pressed his softening cock inward as the cum he'd deposited started leaking out. "I don't know about forever, but I love holding you after sex."

"Wow, you're just slinging that 'L' word around now, aren't you? I love snuggling, too. And I love your cum leaking down my crack."

Shane chuckled. "You're a kinky little shit."

"Yeah, takes one to know one. Besides, you'll help me clean my good chaps. I can't believe you fucked the load out of me."

"I can't believe how loud you screamed. The people next door heard it."

"Fuck it. Fuck them. Just cuddle with me and let me enjoy the best sex I've ever had."

* * * *

The next morning Dustin went with Shane to Todd's hospital room just after breakfast. Todd was in his wheelchair, an ornery expression plastered across his face. That meant he had something he could tease at least one of them about. Judging from the size of the grin when he glanced at Dustin, this was a doozy and probably aimed at him.

"Hey, you look a lot better than the last time I saw you," Dustin said.

"Yeah, you, too. I understand you lost by a few dollars, but you rode Diablo. It was worth it to give up the sponge baths from cute nurses to see you ride him."

Dustin shrugged. "Yeah, but I've already got a ton of sponsors, so next year I'll have a better shot at it."

"Yeah, whatever. Next year I'll beat your ass like a drum."

"Whatever." Dustin leaned down and grabbed Todd in a hug. "I'm glad you're getting out of here."

Todd returned the squeeze with equal ferocity. Then he grinned and pushed Dustin back. "Hey, what the hell? I ain't one of your lover boys like the big dude there."

Shane stepped closer to Dustin and the two shared a quick kiss.

"Eww, get a room!" Todd laughed. "Speaking of rooms, I heard you two went at each other like wet cats last night."

Dustin raised an eyebrow. "What are you talking about?"

"I got a couple of texts about you being a screamer."

Shane's face flushed red, but Dustin shrugged. "If you ever make love that's as good as last night was, you'll scream, too."

Epilogue

Nine months later

Shane ambled back and forth in the nursery, rocking the baby in his arms. He beamed down at his nephew's sleeping face. "Hey, kid, you're awfully cute. I'm your Uncle Shane. You're so worth the crazy drive across all those states to see you born." Shane smiled at Sam with tears pooling in his eyes. "He's so perfect. Blond hair and blue eyes. Tiny little fingers and toes."

"Yeah, they come with all the parts. The doc said the hair and eyes could get darker, but since you have blue eyes and Angie has blue eyes — well, there's a good chance he'll keep them."

"He's the spitting image of you, little brother. You'll be a great dad."

"Yeah, I hope I don't fuck up." Sam glanced around the room. "I mean mess up."

Dustin walked behind them and poked Sam in the ribs. "No more potty mouth for the new dad."

"Yeah, his Uncle Dustin better watch his mouth, too, because this boy's mom and grandma can pack a punch."

"No worries. I can watch my fucking mouth." Dustin turned red. "I'm still working on it."

"So, what's the plan for you two?" Sam asked.

Shane shrugged as he glanced through the living room window at the West Texas landscape. "In a few years, we'd like to buy a small ranch and raise bucking stock. But for now, Dustin's got some top-notch sponsors. He's going to take a run at Nationals again. We're traveling together, but some of the rodeos aren't too sure about having an engaged bull rider and bullfighter in the ring together."

Dustin drew Shane against him and kissed his cheek. "Soon. It'll come soon. We have plenty of time to plan the wedding."

Shane studied the sleeping face of the baby in his arms. "By the time he's grown, I hope the whole discussion about who you can marry will have disappeared. I hope people get to where it doesn't matter who he falls for, so long as they love each other."

The baby twisted in Shane's hands and threw up both arms like a football player who'd just run the winning touchdown into the end zone, then he let out an impressive burp. "He's practicing his Uncle Dustin's dismount."

Dustin rubbed his finger over the baby's hand. The little fellow grabbed Dustin and held on tight. He glanced at Sam. "Look at that grip! He'll be ready to ride his first sheep in no time."

Sam rubbed his hands over his face. "Aww, shit…"

Want to see more from this author?
Here's a taster for you to enjoy!

Leather and Grit:
Wrestling with Destiny
Jon Keys

Excerpt

Tyler struggled to settle his nerves. This was the biggest rodeo he'd participated in since graduating from college and deciding to go for the National Finals. It wasn't a choice he'd made lightly, but the state-of-the-art rig his mother had given him when he'd graduated had made the decision easier. *It's a sweet setup for Rusty and I both.*

As if his horse knew that thoughts of him passed through Tyler's mind, Rusty pressed against his owner, and with great care, put his hoof on top of Tyler's boot and leaned toward the cowboy.

Tyler yelped and shoved on the big gelding. "Damn you! Get off my foot! Ahh!"

Everett chuckled. As Tyler's hazer, he kept the steer from running the wrong direction while Tyler jumped from his horse. Close to ten years older than Tyler, Everett had only worked with him since the start of the season. Tyler didn't have the option of continuing to compete with his college partner. Chuck had two more years before he'd graduate and his father had made it very clear that if Tyler talked his son into quitting school, he'd beat Tyler like a drum.

Tyler had seen it as a serious threat and made sure to discourage any ideas Chuck'd had along those lines. His college rodeo coach had suggested Everett. While not the most congenial partner on the tour, he did his job well. Just as important, Tyler being gay hadn't seemed to be an issue.

Rusty shifted his weight enough for Tyler to jerk his foot out, and Everett commented, "You've let that animal think for himself far too much. He'll dump you one of these days."

Tyler laughed at the idea as he did his usual pre-run check of his equipment. The horse behaved while Tyler tugged the cinch tight. But on his second pull, an ominous pop filled the room.

"What the hell?"

Tyler ran his hands along both sides of the strap. When the first pass found nothing, he calmed himself enough to give the strap a more detailed evaluation.

There it is, past the buckle. A weak spot.

"Something's wrong with the saddle. I'll be back in a sec," he told Everett as he led his mount out of the holding pen. He moved at a fast walk until they'd cleared the crowd then dropped into a sprint toward the trailer. His spare tack supply was extensive, and it only took a few minutes to replace it.

He untied the horse, swung into the saddle and urged Rusty into a gallop. He slowed when he neared the entry, but his rapid pace still earned him a paint-peeling glare from the guy serving as gateman. He brought Rusty to a stop at Everett's flank, and his hazer turned with a raised eyebrow. "I started to think we were giving up."

Tyler shifted back and forth until he knew the new equipment was in good shape. He finished as they were called to the arena. He rode Rusty to the left-side box that had seen more than its share of wear over the decades and his horse banged into it a few times as the excitement grew. Tyler settled the gelding into the box's far corner, and once every detail satisfied him, he nodded for the steer's release.

The rangy red-and-white-mottled animal shot through the open space like a West Texas jackrabbit. But Tyler had dealt with animals similar to this daily for the last ten years.

Already straining to close the interval, he urged Rusty to the short-distance speed bred into the quarter horse. A second later they raced beside the steer. Tyler made all the last second changes and urged a burst of speed from his mount before launching himself.

Tyler equated the instant of weightlessness when he was off his mount to an eagle soaring above its prey. In his mind, the flight lasted less than a thump of his pounding heart. His fantasy burst when he landed on the animal and slammed to the reality of sweat, dirt and racing beef.

He curled his muscular arm around one of its short, thick horns. The other arm snaked its way to the muzzle and Tyler dug his boots into the dry powder under them.

Focused on a single task, he torqued his body, bringing into use every muscle developed over the years. When he twisted the animal around, there was an instant when everything froze in place as the final scene of the drama unfolded with the two gladiators straining to defeat each other.

With a final effort, Tyler won the battle and the steer rolled to its back. An instant later, the crowd erupted in a roar as the judge declared his run ended.

He released the steer, climbed to his feet and used his hat to knock off some of the dust covering his body. He smiled when Everett rode close and held out Rusty's reins. "Good run, kid. Your luck is holding."

Tyler listened as the emcee announced his time. Afterward, he turned to Everett with a broad smile. "Four-point-eight. I'm feeling like a winner tonight." He mounted Rusty to follow Everett to the staging pens then to their trailers. Everett unsaddled his own horse and had her loaded almost before Tyler dismounted. He locked his trailer shut and flashed Tyler a wave. "Later. See ya next weekend."

Before Tyler could do more than return the wave, Everett had left the fairground and disappeared behind a boiling cloud of dust. He waited for the clue to gaining a better understanding of his hazer and his lack of warmth, but after considering it for a few seconds, he shook his head at the reoccurring issue. Tyler considered himself good at making people feel comfortable, but his skill seemed to be ineffective with Everett. Knowing he might never understand the man, he turned to unsaddle Rusty. He was in no particular rush. His next destination was home and nothing urged him to hurry his return.

He tugged off his saddle and tossed it onto a rack. He brushed Rusty until the horse leaned into each stroke then loaded him into the trailer and used the last of the evening sun to see if he could tell what had happened to his original saddle. He tugged the damaged tack into the light and checked the leather inch-by-inch but revealed nothing new. The front cinch had developed a thin crease that weakened with each movement.

He leaned against the trailer and laughed when a dark red muzzle appeared. Tyler scratched the horse's nose as he tried to figure out why the weakness had developed in the cinch. With a final sigh, he pushed off the trailer and readied everything for their trip home. He didn't have a clue what was causing the issue with his equipment but he knew its investigation couldn't be delayed for long.

* * * *

Micah drove the utility vehicle into the welcome shade of the tool shed and sighed. *What a long day.* He was making progress on the fence replacement, but on some days, it felt as if his progress could be measured in inches. He stared at the leather gloves that were becoming flayed from the miles of barbed wire redone so far this spring. But, in reality, he had been productive. Today he'd managed to finish an entire section of fencing, giving Micah a sense of accomplishment on what seemed to be a never-ending task of keeping the ranch operational. As he unloaded the tools and materials from the job, the two blue heelers who were the working dogs for their ranch threw themselves into the shade. He reached down to give each of them a loving scratch behind their ears. "Get some rest, guys. You were good company this afternoon, but we have a lot more to go this summer." Smiling at the familiar interaction, he turned back to his work.

"How'd it go this afternoon?"

Micah sighed at hearing his father's voice. He put the fencing pliers onto the pegboard and turned to his dad. "Good. Got a lot done. I finished repairing the section of fence that butts up against the old Parker place.

Everything should be finished this summer. I need to stop by the Lang ranch and talk to them. I want to confirm they'll be willing to help with the shared fencing."

His father chuckled. "Mary Lou won't let you anywhere close to her precious horses with your barbed wire."

He shook his head. "I ran into Lee in the feed store the other day. We'll do vinyl fencing, so there shouldn't be any issues."

"Isn't the Lang boy back from college?"

Micah hesitated to say anything. His dad was too good at reading his thoughts and his infatuation with Tyler Lang was a secret he would prefer to keep to himself. Tyler's muscular body had provided Micah with jack-off fantasies since they'd been in high school. Now his fantasy man was one of the highest-ranked steer wrestlers in the country. There was no way any of those daydreams would come to life. Besides, he couldn't bear the thought of how his dad would react if Micah came out as gay. He couldn't see it happening.

"Micah? Everything okay?"

He dropped the pointless speculation and answered the question. "Someone told me he was back in town. They said he is Grand Marshall for the Fourth of July parade, but I haven't seen him."

His dad frowned. "You work too hard. Take some time off and enjoy yourself. You don't have to finish all the things on your list every day."

Micah made a final check that he'd put everything into its place before turning to his father. "Well, if it will make you feel any better, I planned to go to the rodeo tonight. Dustin Lewis is one of the bull riders. From what I've seen, he's doing better this year. He has a good chance of winning at Nationals."

"Isn't that the boy who's married to another man?"

Micah swallowed hard. "Yeah, he's with Shane Rees, the bullfighter. I don't know if they're married or not."

It was impossible for Micah to interpret his father's expression, but he seemed to be thinking about the information. Then he turned to Micah. "Good. I hope you enjoy yourself. You've earned a break from all the work. Go clean up. I'll feed and water the stock." He waved his hand at Micah as his grin got even larger. "If you don't make it home before dawn, I'll take care of everything then, too."

Micah snorted. "Yeah, like that would ever happen. I'll take care of the animals in the morning. But if you'd do the evening feeding, I wouldn't mind getting to the fairground in time to see everything before the rodeo begins."

He waved Micah toward the house. "Go get ready. I can handle a few old hens and a lazy bull."

"Thanks, Dad. I'll tell you all about it tomorrow."

A short time later, Micah sat on the bench in the entryway, pulling off his boots before moving into his room. In the dim, cool bedroom he had no trouble smelling the odor from a day of hard work. He wrinkled his nose as he stripped off the last of his clothing and dropped it all into the hamper. After a relaxing stretch, Micah turned on the shower and adjusted the spray until it was hot enough to begin relaxing his stiff muscles. He stepped inside, the water cascading over his neck, and he moaned. After letting the water wet him thoroughly, Micah soaped himself. He thought about Tyler as his body responded to the fantasy. He teased his soap-covered hand up and down his dick, enjoying the sensation on his now-iron-hard shaft.

Steam filled the glass enclosure as Micah lost himself in the pleasure. He ran his fist up and down his cock as he explored his taut body with his other hand. A minute later, he leaned against the shower wall as he pounded his shaft, his breath coming in gasps. As he tensed with orgasm, he twisted his nipple and sent himself over the edge.

His climax painted the glass door with white lines as he shook with pleasure. With his balls tight against his erupting cock, Micah enjoyed the waves of ecstasy washing over him. He stripped the final strands of cum from his softening dick until he was focused on more than his trembling muscles.

As the last of the sexual euphoria left his body, he stepped back under the cascade to finish his shower. A short time later, he was done and used one of the plush towels to dry himself. He dropped the damp towel into the clothes hamper, walked into the bedroom and went through his closet to look for something to wear. He made his typical choice of pressed Wranglers, a heavy western shirt and boots polished to within an inch of their lives. It was likely he'd run into someone he knew and he planned on being prepared.

Once he had everything in place, including the addition of a tooled leather belt, he checked his appearance in the full-length mirror hanging from the closet door. Satisfied with what he saw, Micah headed out to the fairgrounds.

Sign up for our newsletter and find out about all our romance book releases, eBook sales and promotions, sneak peeks and FREE romance books!

About the Author

Jon Keys' earliest memories revolve around books; with the first ones he can recall reading himself being "The Warlord of Mars" and anything with Tarzan. (The local library wasn't particularly up to date.) But as puberty set in, he started sneaking his mother's romance magazines and added the world of romance and erotica to his mix of science fiction, fantasy, Native American, westerns and comic books.

A voracious reader for almost half a century, Jon has only recently begun creating his own flights of fiction for the entertainment of others. Born in the Southwest and now living in the Midwest, Jon has worked as a ranch hand, teacher, computer tech, roughneck, designer, retail clerk, welder, artist, and, yes, pool boy; with interests ranging from kayaking and hunting to painting and cooking, he draws from a wide range of life experiences to create written works that draw the reader in and wrap them in a good story.

Jon loves to hear from readers. You can find his contact information, website details and author profile page at https://www.pride-publishing.com